A DOUBLE LIFE

RUSSIAN LIBRARY

R

The Russian Library at Columbia University Press publishes an expansive selection of Russian literature in English translation, concentrating on works previously unavailable in English and those ripe for new translations. Works of premodern, modern, and contemporary literature are featured, including recent writing. The series seeks to demonstrate the breadth, surprising variety, and global importance of the Russian literary tradition and includes not only novels but also short stories, plays, poetry, memoirs, creative nonfiction, and works of mixed or fluid genre.

■ □ ■

For a complete list of books in the series, see page 139.

KAROLINA

A DOUBLE LIFE

PAVLOVA

Translated and with an
introduction by Barbara Heldt

Columbia University Press New York

Published with the support of Read Russia, Inc.,
     and the Institute of Literary Translation, Russia
Columbia University Press
Publishers Since 1893
New York   Chichester, West Sussex
cup.columbia.edu

Library of Congress Cataloging-in-Publication Data
Names: Pavlova, Karolina, 1807–1893, author. | Heldt, Barbara,
     1940– translator, writer of introduction.
Title: A double life / Karolina Pavlova ; translated and with an
     introduction by Barbara Heldt.
Other titles: Dvoĭnaia zhizn'. English (Heldt)
Description: New York : Columbia University Press, 2019. |
     Series: Russian library
Identifiers: LCCN 2018054278 (print) | LCCN 2018058345 (ebook) |
     ISBN 9780231549110 (electronic) | ISBN 9780231190787 (cloth : alk.
     paper) | ISBN 9780231190794 (pbk.)
Classification: LCC PG3337.P35 (ebook) | LCC PG3337.P35 D8613 2019
     (print) | DDC 893.71/3—dc 3
LC record available at https://lccn.loc.gov/2018054278

Columbia University Press books are printed on permanent
     and durable acid-free paper.
Printed in the United States of America

Cover design: Roberto de Vicq de Cumptich
Book design: Lisa Hamm

CONTENTS

INTRODUCTION

Karolina Pavlova: The Woman Poet and the Double Life

BARBARA HELDT

In the nineteenth century, when its literature equaled that written at any place at any time in history, Russia had no "great" woman writer—no Sappho, no Ono, no Komachi or Murasaki Shikibu, no Madame de Staël or George Sand, no Jane Austen or George Eliot—or so we might say when surveying the best-known works of the age. But we now know this truth to be less than true.

Karolina Pavlova, born Karolina Karlovna Jaenisch in Yaroslavl in 1807, died in Dresden in 1893 after having lived outside Russia for four decades. She had abandoned her native country not because of tsarist oppression but because of hostile criticism of her poetry and her personal life. She died without friends, without family, without money, without renown (not a single Russian newspaper gave her an obituary)[1] but with an unyielding dedication to what she called her "holy craft," which had produced a body of fine literary, largely poetic, works.

In 1848, when she had completed her only novel, *A Double Life*, Pavlova was not only devoted to art but also enjoyed other, more transient pleasures like love, friendship, and respect, which she was to lose later on. To judge from the irony that pervades her otherwise romantic description in this book of a young girl who has everything, Karolina Pavlova even at that time had come to expect little from the world beyond what her own talents and personality could bring to it. The theme of conflict between poet and society had informed the works of the great lyric poets who were her predecessors, Alexander Pushkin and Mikhail Lermontov.

Pavlova returned to this theme again and again, translating her emotions into verse of abstract classical precision, which her detractors called cold, heartless, and remote from the so-called real problems of life. Even when there was admiration for her poetry, it was mixed with ridicule of her personally. Thus, a letter of her fellow poet N.M. Iazykov in 1832[2] contains hints that this extraordinary phenomenon, a woman poet, was somehow ridiculous when reciting her poetry, as was then the custom. In this way was engendered a more subtle conflict than that of poet versus society—that of woman poet versus society and ultimately, of woman versus poet within Pavlova herself.

As much as any woman of her time could in Russia, Pavlova lived in a man's world. Her father, Karl Jaenisch, was a professor of physics and chemistry at the School of Medicine and Surgery in Moscow; many university professors in Russia were, like him, of German origin. Jaenisch adored his daughter and saw to it that she received a superb education at home—the only place in Russia where a woman could get a higher education (Moscow University was not officially open to women until 1876, although various so-called women's courses existed beginning in the early 1870s). Her first romantic love was the great Polish poet Adam Mickiewicz, who tutored her in Polish (she already knew Russian, French, German, Spanish, Italian, Swedish, and Dutch, as well as Russian) and was stunned by her literary talent. In the late 1820s, Karolina Jaenisch was already attending the important literary gatherings in Moscow, translating poetry, and writing her own works in German and French. In 1833, her first book appeared—a translation of Russian poets into German called *Das Nordlicht*.

In December 1836, she married Nikolai Pavlov, a minor figure in the world of letters whose talent soon ran dry. Pavlov's friend B.N. Chicherin wrote in his memoirs that Pavlov confessed to having married Karolina for her money—"a social misdemeanor," Chicherin says, "that is quite usual and looked upon with indulgence."[3]

On Thursdays in their Moscow house from 1839 to 1844, the leading figures of the day attended the Pavlovs' literary salon.[4] Poets would read aloud from their latest works, and the exponents of the two social philosophies of the age, the Slavophiles and the Westernizers, would gather for sharp debate until their mutual hostility grew too great for social gatherings to countenance. The Pavlovs had a son named Ippolit, who recalled how his mother would often retire from her large and noisy household and compose her verses by speaking them aloud, walking back and forth in her room, repeating, rearranging, and modifying words and phrases.[5]

An alien figure both because she was perceived as being "German" and because she was a woman-poet, Pavlova lived above all for her art. The recurrent theme in her relationships with all her famous contemporaries is her need, through their friendship, to confirm her view of herself as a poet. In poetry dedicated to them, she constantly reiterates what she wrote to Yevgeny Baratynsky in 1842: "You have called me poet, / Liking my careless verse; / And I, warmed by your light, / Believed, then, in myself."

But circumstances of her life conspired to undermine this belief. If Pavlov married Karolina for her money, he soon began to gamble it away, sometimes at the rate of 10,000 to 15,000 rubles in an evening. Friends noticed that as her literary fame increased and his declined, he grew jealous: "Soon her poetry will be read more than his short stories. It seems he fears this."[6] Pavlov set up a separate household with a younger cousin of his wife, whom Karolina had taken in and helped support.

The loneliness of Pavlova's position was greatly intensified by the fact that, despite the long list of famous men among her acquaintances, most of her male contemporaries disliked her intensely and interpreted her shaky pride as haughtiness, and her love of poetry as theatrical posing. As a Soviet scholar has written: "The ironic references to Karolina Jaenisch are as frequent as the well-wishing ones, if not more frequent, and the latter in their tone . . . invariably include a shade of irony and mockery. The number of epigrams aimed at Jaenisch appear not less in number than the number of album verses full of praise and ecstasy."[7] To many, Pavlova's claim to live only for her art seemed a monstrous thing in a woman—or at best something to be indulgently patronized.

From I. I. Panaev, the powerful editor and minor writer and publicist, comes the most consistently unfavorable picture of her. He claims to have felt "timidity" in her presence:

> Before me was a tall, extremely thin lady, stern and majestic in appearance . . . In her pose, in her glance was something affected, rhetorical. She stopped between two marble columns, with dignity she inclined her head slightly at my bow and then extended her hand to me with the majesty of a theatrical empress. . . . Within five minutes I learned from Mrs. Pavlov that she had received much attention from Alexander [von] Humboldt and Goethe—and the latter had

written some lines to her in her album . . . then the album with these precious pages was brought forth. . . . Within a quarter of an hour Karolina Karlovna was declaiming to me some verses translated by her from German and English.[8]

By drawing attention to her work, promoting it to an influential man of letters, Pavlova may have thought that she was acting in the normal professional manner, but this way of *being a poet* was perceived as grotesque in a female. Panaev also relates that Pavlova treated her husband rudely (as well she might have, considering that by then, Nikolai was gambling away her entire estate). Panaev, too, seems to be responsible for the glib slanders against Pavlova's verse, which followed naturally from his dislike of her personally. Once, when Timofey Granovsky began to praise her poetry, Panaev set him straight by reading a parody of Pavlova, and from then on, or so he claims, Granovsky had nothing further to do with her.

Panaev's poem, like all his "parodies," is actually a satire directing itself at Pavlova's person, rather than an attempt to imitate parodically the qualities of her verse. Another and more genuine parody of Pavlova, called "My Disillusionment," by another critic on the left, the poet Nikolay Nekrasov, bemoans the possibility that women might want to give up jelly-boiling and pickle-making for philosophy and literature. One can only regret that Nekrasov, who often expressed in his poetry a voyeuristic sympathy for "fallen women" (as prostitutes of the time were romantically called), was incapable of extending the same sympathy to women of his own class.

D. V. Grigorovich, in his memoirs, repeats a common criticism of Pavlova's poetry which, because it was untrue, seemed to stem from both ideological and personal dislike. He says that when they were introduced, "not half an hour had gone by after the customary courtesies but she was already reading to me and the two or three other people sitting there her verses, which are distinguished more by the beautiful sounds of the words than the poetic content."[9] This criticism of her verse—that it subordinated sense to sound—reflects a common charge made by poets and critics of utilitarian persuasion against those of either the Slavophile or the "art for art's sake" philosophy. Panaev and the crusading journal *The Contemporary* were Pavlova's opponents in an intellectually polarized Russia, and she in turn condemned the utilitarians as "cold minds" (in her "Poslanie I. S. Aksakovu" of 1846).

Even Pavlova's literary friends wrote, if not articles and memoirs, then private letters condemning her as a woman. The Slavophiles appreciated Pavlova as a poet not only for the nationalist content of some of her verses but also for making Russian poetry known abroad through her translations. Yet when Pavlova finally took matters in hand and initiated proceedings that led to her husband's arrest after he mortgaged her property in secret, even her closest friends turned against her. She could not have foreseen that Pavlov's reputation as a liberal would bring about a search of his library, which contained some banned books; as a result of this discovery, he was jailed and sentenced to a ten-month exile in Perm. He was later pardoned by the authorities and returned to live with his wife's cousin, but their friends never forgave Pavlova.

During the early months of 1853, Pavlova wrote nothing. She left for Petersburg, where her father died in a cholera epidemic. Trying to avoid contagion, she left without attending his burial, and a new scandal arose because of her treatment of the dead man. In May 1853, she settled in Dorpat with her son and mother. In the midst of her distress, she met a law student named Boris Utin, twenty-five years younger than she, who became the profoundest love of her life. Her long poetic silence was broken in January 1854 with a poem that celebrated their meeting and the rare relationship of equals that Pavlova needed to have with men. It contains a double tension. The first is that of two people communicating while at the same time participating in society games (Pavlova does not indulge in a Byronic rejection of society; she describes the even-more-difficult triumph of feeling within its context). The second is that between two people themselves as they experience, fight, and resolve a complete sexual and spiritual attraction. Initially as enemies, and finally as brothers, they are always equals:

Strange, the way we met. In a drawing-room circle
  With its empty conversation,
Almost furtively, not knowing one another,
  We guessed at our kinship.

And we realized our souls' likeness
  Not by passionate words tumbling at random from our lips,
But by mind answering mind,
  And the gleam of hidden thoughts.

Diligently absorbed by modish nonsense,
  Uttering witty remarks,
We suddenly looked at each other
  With a curious, attentive glance,

And each of us, successfully fooling them all
  With our chatter and joking,
Heard in the other the arrogant, terrible
  Laughter of the Spartan boy.

And, meeting, we did not try to find
  In the other's soul an echo of our own.
All evening the two of us spoke stiffly,
  Locking up our sadness.

Not knowing whether we would meet again,
  Meeting unexpectedly that evening,
With strange truthfulness, cruelly, sternly,
  We waged war until morning.

Abusing every habitual notion,
  Like foe with merciless foe,
Silently and firmly, like brothers,
  Later we shook hands.

In February 1854, Pavlova's son, Ippolit, went back to Russia to live with his father and attend university the following year. Pavlova settled in Dresden in 1858 and remained there for the rest of her life—in exile from the language in which she wrote, from the poetic tradition that she had admirably continued, and from the country and the city she loved, scorned by the prominent people she had known best, who at their best were her literary peers.

Pavlova continued writing. She reminds one of George Sand, who worked eight hours a day regardless of the emotional turmoil in her life. One of Pavlova's former literary friends, Ivan Aksakov, visited her in 1860 in Dresden, where she was living on a strict budget. Aksakov chose to give a negative interpretation to what might have been a refusal to let her grim life drag her under:

> She, of course, was extremely happy to see me, but within ten minutes, even less, was already reading her verse to me. . . . She is completely bold, merry, happy, self-satisfied to a high degree, and occupied only with herself. This is such a curious psychological subject, it should be studied. It would seem that the catastrophe which has befallen her, a true misfortune experienced by her, the separation from her son, loss of her place in society, name and wealth, her poverty, the necessity of living by her labors—all this, it would seem, would strongly shake a person, leave profound traces on him . . . nothing of the sort, she is the same as always, has not changed at all except that she has grown older and everything that has happened to her has only served as material for her verses. . . . It's astonishing! In this woman filled with talent, everything is rubbish—there is nothing serious, profound, true, and sincere—at bottom there is an awful heartlessness, a dullness, a lack of development. Her sincerity of soul exists only in the form of art, all of it has gone into poetry, into verse, instead of feeling there is a sort of external exaltation. You feel that, of course, she herself does not realize that she loves no one, that for her nothing is cherished, dear, holy.[10]

Aksakov adds that she is "poisoned by Art." Strength of character thus becomes weakness or disease.

The riddle of Pavlova's nature that Aksakov puts forward seems to be easily solvable. Her quickness to declaim her verses, her strident living for her craft alone that is so emphatically noticed by all the sources quoted, can be seen as another kind of attempt to prove to herself that despite her womanhood, she was indeed a serious poet, not a mere salon hostess—a poetry-writing woman, as most of her more gifted female predecessors in Russia had been.

At times, the effort of being both poet and woman led to a split between Pavlova's poetic philosophy and her philosophy of life—a double life of the spirit. In the same letter, Aksakov writes of Pavlova: "She will tell you that she no longer believes in human friendship— and it's all nonsense, and within five minutes in her poetry, excellent poetry, she boasts that she has preserved her faith in friendship and in people."

These accusations, voiced or rumored, of contradictory, almost hypocritical emotions or "dryness of heart," as Chicherin put it, had an effect on Pavlova that is best seen in her actual work. Pavlova's own writings give a very different picture from that of a woman sure of her art and cold to life.

Her friends did try to reassure Pavlova that, within the conventions of her time, she was free to write. We have a report from Ivan Aksakov's sister, quoted in one of his 1860 letters, that "Karolina Karlovna is upset and says that poetry is not a serious occupation and she is looking for a serious occupation." Aksakov's sister tells him to reassure Pavlova that "the chief business of her life is the education of her son and her maternal calling," and because these are assured, "she can without pangs of conscience devote herself to occupations not serious."[11] One can imagine how consoling this advice from a typical, well-meaning woman of her circle must have been to Pavlova.

The harsh criticism of her poetry in *The Contemporary* led Pavlova to write a long, rambling letter to Panaev, full of deprecation of both her sex and her art. However grand their tone, the following words show that Pavlova's doubts and hesitations always took the form of questioning herself as a *woman* poet:

> It is said that the chief content of a woman's letter is in the postscript: I give you new proof of the truth of this pronouncement; only at the end of my letter do I decide to utter what is foremost in my heart, that your criticisms cut me to the quick. I do not repudiate my sex and have not conquered its weaknesses; whatever you may say, a woman-poet always remains more woman than poet and authorial egotism in her is weaker than female egotism. . . . I have never wished nor tried to make myself an author; this necessity that exists in me for better or for worse, this calling I keep in check as much as I can.[12]

Thus, Pavlova tries to defend her innocence; to wit, she is guilty only of the petty vanity of women, not the colossal vanity of a woman who wants to be a poet. She apologizes for her talent to the man who edited the most powerful journal of the time, but, as we have seen, in vain.

In exile, Pavlova came to view life as a challenge to survive. As she wrote to Olga Kireeva from Dresden on July 22, 1860, when alone and beset by financial difficulties, "I am occupied with the contemplation of an interesting experiment; I wish to see whether everything that befalls me will strengthen me; whether I will withstand it or not."[13] But even in exile, Pavlova, who was never closed to life, was able to form her last great literary friendship with a man who treated her not as a monster, but as an admired equal—Aleksey Konstantinovich Tolstoy, the poet, playwright, and humorist. They met in Dresden in 1860, and she translated his poetry and plays into

German so that they could be acclaimed outside his native country. As his letters show, she also helped him with the Russian originals.[14] He in turn secured a pension for her from the Russian government and corresponded warmly and solicitously with her until his death in 1875. Pavlova outlived him by eighteen years and died worse than reviled—she died utterly forgotten.

II

To be more than charitable, we might say that Pavlova's life and art were so badly misread by her contemporaries because she was such a unique phenomenon in Russia. The eminent scholar B. Ya. Bukhshtab writes of how the first century of the new Russian poetry, from 1740–1840 approximately, brought forth not one notable woman author.[15] Pavlova's only contemporary female poet of note, the Countess Evdokiia Rostopchina, was as different from Pavlova as were the cities in which they lived, St. Petersburg and Moscow. Rostopchina's poetry, aside from being stylistically less interesting than Pavlova's, reads more like a chronicle of her vastly more successful life. This more intimate, domestic sort of poetry ("I am only a woman . . . ready to be proud of this," Rostopchina wrote in her lyric "Temptation") was and is generally considered peculiarly appropriate to women writers. Pavlova's own verse—its feeling restrained, and lyric meditation or elegy being her preferred genre—was considered by her contemporaries, as it was by the modern Russian poet Vladislav Khodasevich, as "above all not feminine."[16] Pavlova's lyrics, such as the cycle of poems inspired by her love for Boris Utin, can hardly be termed cold or abstract, but even when her poems reflect personal emotion, the feeling is both intensified and generalized, as is true in the case of most good poetry.

Neither Pavlova's longer poems nor her prose works present a kind of confessional; still, her treatment of the theme of woman is central to many of them. Here as well, she was able to turn from the exact circumstances of her own life to the whole condition of the lives of others like her, the Russian women of her class. (Pavlova has no illusions about an aristocrat really being able to fathom the depths of misery of Russia's poor, and she mocks Cecily, the heroine of *A Double Life*, for thinking that poverty can somehow be graceful.)

Until recently, Pavlova's works were never discussed critically in terms of the primary theme that would link them to her life. Critics of both her and our times have pretended that her treatment of women is no more than a mere aspect of a criticism of aristocratic Russian society in general. But especially in a few of her longer poems and in her prose works, Pavlova concerned herself in a primary sense with women's "fate"—with *fate* in quotation marks to stress the fact that if her women fail to be the agents of their destiny, it is not because their nature dooms them to suffering, but because the actions of men determine their fate. She described especially keenly the peculiar amorphousness of women's lives, of what is expected and not expected of them, or, as she called it in her long narrative poem "Quadrille," "the confusion (*bestolkovost'*) of woman's role—/ A mixture of willfulness and constraint / Which is nearly always our lot." The willfulness of a young girl who is seemingly free to accept or reject any man she wants and to construct her own dreams of life, as well as the constraint that the narrowness of her upbringing, the rules of acceptable conduct in society, and the ultimate necessity of marriage impose on her, form part of the duality of *A Double Life*.

In some of her other writings, Pavlova described the later stages of a woman's life as well, although she had no definite comprehensive plans to be complete in this respect. In "Quadrille," published in 1859 but begun as early as 1843, four women who are already married tell each other their stories, recalling how in different ways, their girlish illusions have been shattered. In her memoirs, which survive only in the fragment that was published in 1877, Pavlova, in the midst of a description of her own happy childhood, gives us a portrait of the death of a very old lady, a creature from a previous age. Again, we see the paradoxical quality of a woman's existence—bound by convention, yet full of strange, heroic independence. The old lady has nursed a breast cancer without telling anyone about it: "This pampered lady to whom the smallest inconvenience was a burden, suffered a tormenting pain over the years, without permitting herself a single outcry." She would lock herself in her bedroom and wash the blood and pus from her underwear so that even her maid would not see it. Pavlova's father, who had a medical degree, was a close friend of this woman and suspected nothing. Pavlova expands the paradox:

> Seeing a doctor every day, in whose art she fully believed, she had the strength of spirit not to betray herself even once, not to ask for help or the alleviation of the disease which was killing her! And all from modesty, in order not to have to bare her breast before a doctor—the breast of a sixty-year-old woman! One can call that folly, but it is impossible not to recognize a heroism of sorts in a woman who, awaiting an inescapably near and agonizing death, to the very end did not allow herself the merest slight to decorum, the most negligible digression from accustomed rules, did not once

forget to embellish her clothes with the appropriate ribbon, to rouge her cheeks, and affix a mouche to her face.[17]

This strange behavior is the logical result of the upbringing to which young girls were subjected—and a true story stranger than any fiction. Russian realism had to pretend to have a semblance of believability; Russian reality did not.

While Pavlova felt a generalized sympathy with all the ages of woman, all "mute sisters of my soul," as she called them in her dedicatory poem to *A Double Life*, she still felt closest to people of keen intelligence and to poets. Most of her heroines are not she. Like Cecily in *A Double Life*, their talents are unconscious, suppressed by circumstances of their lives as Pavlova never allowed hers to be. A long story of 1859 called "At the Tea-Table"[18] begins with a sharp debate about the lack of equality of the sexes and whether women's dependency and inferiority are inevitable. One character asserts that women are educated to be childlike and then politely scorned for having childish minds; another says that a woman's nature is different from a man's. Later, a story within the story is told, and its main character, the Countess Aline, says to a man who wants to marry her: "Don't you know that to praise a woman's intelligence means to reprove her? Aren't people all convinced that there is no heart? Hasn't it been decided that an intelligent woman is some kind of monster that has no feelings? Ask anyone; anyone will tell you this." Pavlova's own bitterness emerges at times, untransmuted by the more generalized passion of her art.

While Pavlova was nearly alone among Russian women writers of her time in the realization of her ambition to be a poet of importance, she was also part of the beginning of a new kind of literary activity in Russia—one concerning women and often involving women writers. In the second third of the nineteenth century, while women were beginning to write in the popular journals of the day, critics eagerly debated whether women should or should not write, and what was women's special sphere of talent as writers. Related to this phenomenon was the fact that in the 1830s, male writers were developing the possibility of the society tale for social criticism and psychological intrigue. Still earlier, in France, Madame de Genlis had perfected this genre. In her story "La Femme Auteur," she even confronts this problem of the woman writer: "Men would never accept a woman author as an equal; they would be more jealous of her than of a man."[19]

In Russia, Vladimir Odoevsky refined this genre in the 1830s, and stories like his "Princess Mimi" (1834) and "Princess Zizi" (1839) have as their central figures independent, contradictory women who manipulate, if not their own destinies, then certainly those of others. If their lives produce evil results, then Odoevsky lets us know that their education is to blame: "They teach [a girl] dancing, drawing, and music so that she may get married. . . . This is the beginning and end of her life. It *is* her life."

Lermontov sees the same social types, but much more from the man's point of view. In "Princess Ligovskaya" (1836), which formed the basis for part of *A Hero of Our Time*, the main character is one who is hurt by society, and women, whether unyielding ("the class of women who have no heart") or vulnerable, are damned either way. For women, says Lermontov, "tears are a weapon both for offense and for defense."

A third author of society tales, V. A. Sollogub, wrote at least one piece that probably had some influence on *A Double Life*, a story called *The Ball*. It describes how men and women both hide their feelings behind masks. In a dream, their real emotions surface but only temporarily. The narrator is a man, but the woman he loves/ hates has a long confessional monologue. Thus, for a decade before Pavlova wrote *A Double Life*, the prose writers of Russia were describing, with varying degrees of sympathy, women in society whose conflict with the world took place in the shrunken arenas of their townhouses, in their drawing rooms, behind their tea tables. In these small places where they fought the determining battles of their lives, their strength is tested and their character defined as surely and dramatically as if they, like the men, had gone to the rugged mountains or limitless horizons of the Caucasus to pacify the natives and fight duels with fellow officers.

The publication of *A Double Life* in 1848, when Pavlova was at the height of her fame as a poet and translator, was a literary event that drew the attention of all the important literary journals of Russia. One chapter of the novel had been published a year before, and the full work was eagerly anticipated. The fact that it was part prose and part poetry seemed to bother no one; the reviewers understood the purpose of this structure and praised the quality of the poetry highly. Even *The Contemporary's* anonymous reviewer called Pavlova's new work "original in form, in the highest degree remarkable in content."[20] In one of the peculiar tributes to which women poets are subject, he stated that the poetry was so sharp and energetic that "it is difficult to recognize in it the tender hand of woman." Showing his social conscience, he praised Pavlova for dealing with important questions like the education of society women. He also made the crucial distinction that the heroine carries poetry in her soul without actually being a poet. But his enthusiasm went far beyond the text, causing him to utter something contradictory to the ideas of the novel that he had just been praising when he rhapsodized that young girls should certainly not try to lose their love of parties and cease to cultivate feminine charms:

> On the contrary, we would even wish our girls and especially women more of that desire to please. Maybe this would save them from the terrible change which comes over them when they get married, when they no longer consider it necessary to dress nicely at home for their husbands, when they replace the corset with the peignoir, the slender figure with a full body.[21]

Here, the male imagination, indulging in literary and social criticism of a most fanciful kind, itself becomes ex post facto a kind of background for what Pavlova was dealing with in her novel.

A Double Life, a novel in ten chapters, is the story of a young girl named Cecily von Lindenborn, whom we see being trapped into a meaningless life and marriage by the people closest to her—her well-meaning mother; her best friend, Olga; and Olga's mother, an experienced social manipulator. In the last chapter, Dmitry, Cecily's suitor, marries her for money. Pavlova does an excellent job of describing this kind of man of little will, who is teased by his friends into a pledge of faithlessness to his marriage even before it takes place. As one of the bachelors says, "Who would want to get married if the blessed state of matrimony made it necessary to give up wine and good times?" Cecily, on the other hand, has only vague premonitions that something is going wrong. Her upbringing has so carefully cultivated an almost total ignorance that she could never commit the slightest peccadillo . . . could never forget herself for a moment, raise her voice half a tone . . . enjoy a conversation with a man to the point where she might talk to him ten minutes longer than was proper or look to the right when she was supposed to look to the left.

Cecily, surrounded by wealth, friends, and family, is ultimately quite alone. Her mother, who accompanies Cecily almost constantly and communicates with her not at all, wants her married—to someone rich if possible, but married. Her closest friend, Olga, encourages Cecily's marriage, so that she will be *hors concours* for a certain disdainful Prince Victor, who goes off to Paris in the last chapter anyway, and in so doing foils the carefully laid plans of Olga's mother, Natalia Afanasevna Valitskaia. Clever as this prime mover of the intrigue underlying *A Double Life* may be, it is the men who always have the ultimate option of freedom.

Like most of the great Russian novels of its time, this one is set in the aristocratic world. Pavlova further logically restricts her heroine to the female quarters of this world—enclosed and protected in domestic interiors or carriages traveling from house to house or from house to church. In the rare moments when Cecily steps onto a balcony or rides on horseback, she experiences a short-lived sense of exhilaration and of control over fate: "She gave herself over to the joy of riding horseback, to the attractions of this living force, this half-free will that carried her off and that she was guiding." This is Pavlova's most potent sexual metaphor in the nondream sections of the novel—and probably the best that Cecily will be granted before or after her marriage.

Nevertheless, it is in the most secluded place, in her bedroom, that Cecily is the least constrained. Here, we see the revelations of her mind freed from its mental corset (to use Pavlova's image). Every chapter has the same structure, with some variation—a day of society's vanities and cruelties followed by a night of dreams. Each chapter begins in prose and ends in verse, with the verse expressing a kind of interior monologue to reflect the double life that Cecily leads. The sections linking them are often in rhythmical prose and describe a state of drowsing, between reality and dream. There are other links as well: She dreams about people she hears about in the drawing room by day and thinks in her waking hours of what she has seen in her dreams. Finally, dreams and waking have an inverse emotional correlation: the better that Cecily's real life seems to become as her marriage approaches, the greater the anguish expressed in her poetic dreams.

Each separate chapter has its own careful structure as well. The ninth, for example, begins and ends with Cecily's sad dreaming and contrasts in the middle the prewedding parties of bride and groom; the tenth begins in the brilliant but artificial illumination of Cecily's mother's house and ends with the church lights being extinguished after the wedding and a view of the dark, empty street. And there is often a nice alternation of style from one chapter to the next: Chapter 6 contains long, descriptive or ironically didactic paragraphs; Chapter 7 deals with the machinations of Muscovite matrons predominantly in dialogue (as each says the opposite of what she thinks, and the others know it but must pretend to take her words at face value).

Within the well-planned framework of the novel are the equally important small touches—symbolic, ironic, humorous. Pavlova excels in the topography of social relations: who sits near whom and who walks with whom determine whole years of a character's life. The breaking of a blossom or closing of the latch on a jeweled bracelet symbolizes a future life broken and encircled. The most pathetic female character of all is named Nadezhda: she still has (as her name is translated) "hope" that she too will be married someday.

Pavlova, as unabashedly as any of the nineteenth-century male writers that were her contemporaries, makes clear in her fiction her own preferences and values in life. Thus, its attitude toward poetry is the measure of the society of the novel. When a poet suffers and is ridiculed, society is condemned. Even Cecily dares set her creative mind free only in dreams; in her waking life, she knew "that there were even women poets, but this was always presented to her as the most pitiable, abnormal thing, as a disastrous and dangerous illness." The behavior of the two sexes is unequally compared by Pavlova. She describes men posing as carefully as women in society (they are equal in vanity); but her men have a particular crudeness that her women are free of, and some of her women have certain attractive virtues that her men at best only seem to have—"that violent female daring which is so far from manly valor."

Pavlova possesses a romanticism that is characteristic of her time but mixed with an ironic sense of reality. We are told repeatedly that Cecily's love for Dmitry is good even if Dmitry himself is not. Cecily's mysterious sickliness both enhances her worldly beauty and brings her closer to the other world of which she dreams. Cecily is vulnerable like two of the novel's minor characters—the poet who encounters boredom when he recites and the dead wife who is reproached for having loved her husband too well. Nature and seasonal change play an important role, even in this society tale. The sounds of nature outside Cecily's room mark a transition from waking to dreams. Nature acts as an ironic accomplice to society when, in the gardens of a summerhouse, "even nature made itself unnatural."

The starry expanse of sky often provides a contrast to the petty world below. The novel begins in the spring, when Cecily dreams of love, and ends in the autumn, when she is married. The coming winter is strongly implied.

The strength of this novel, as of Pavlova's view of life, is that both merge these romantic concepts into an ultimately clear realism. The countless ironic touches in *A Double Life*—from purely lexical ones, such as the use of the word *satisfied*, to larger metaphors, like the one comparing marriage to a mother pushing her daughter out of the window onto the pavement below—prevent the reader from becoming too lost in the enjoyment of the details of how rich aristocrats live. Similarly, as much as we could wish a happier ending for Cecily, Pavlova leaves her, and us, with the one weapon against life that does not destroy life: consciousness. The double awareness that this is the way things are and ought not to be, and the high quality of Pavlova's narrative and poetic style, are themselves a vivid protest against the destiny of women.

And the first sentence of chapter 1 (" 'But are they rich?' ") is the best opening line of any Russian novel. In Russian, it takes only two words: "*A bogaty?*"

NOTES

1. These and many other biographical facts have been discovered or confirmed by Munir Sendich. See his unpublished dissertation, *The Life and Works of Karolina Pavlova* (New York University, 1968), and his publications of Pavlova's correspondence: "Twelve Unpublished Letters to Alexey Tolstoi," *Russian Literature Triquarterly*, no. 9 (Spring 1974), 541–58, and "Boris Utin in Pavlova's Poems and Correspondence: Pavlova's Unpublished Letters to Utin," *Russian Language Journal* 28, no. 100 (1974): 63–88. The other early Pavlova scholar writing in English cannot resist moralizing, rather obtusely, that it was Pavlova's "serious shortcoming . . . to allow the unhappy trends of her own personal life to intrude

into her work." See Anthony D. Briggs, "Twofold Life: A Mirror of Karolina Pavlova's Shortcomings and Achievement," *Slavonic and East European Review* 49, no. 114 (January 1971): 1–17. Slavic studies have come a bit further since these words were written, but they stand as a monument to past practice.

For the most complete biography of Pavlova, the reader is referred to Diana Greene's entry on her in the *Dictionary of Russian Woman Writers*, ed. Marina Ledkovsky, Charlotte Rosenthal, and Mary Zirin (Westport, CT: Greenwood, 1994), 492–93. Greene's entry predates the excellent discussion of Pavlova and her cultural context in Catriona Kelly, *A History of Women's Writing; 1820–1992* (Oxford: Clarendon Press, 1994), 93–107. See also Greene's "Gender and Genre in Pavlova's *A Double Life*," *Slavic Review* 54, no. 3 (1995): 563–77. Pavlova has yet to have a full-length study devoted to her; the present translation is still the only publication of *Dvoinaia zhizn'* (A Double Life) as a separate book in any language.

A symposium on Karolina Pavlova was held at Wesleyan University in April 1995, resulting in the fullest scholarly publication about her to date: *Essays on Karolina Pavlova*, ed. Susanne Fusso and Alexander Lehrman (Evanston, IL: Northwestern University Press, 2001). Susanne Fusso's contribution to this work, "Pavlova's *Quadrille*: The Feminine Variant of (the End of) Romanticism," explores new ways in which Pavlova's femaleness became a literary fact within her poetic works.

2. N. M. Iazykov, *Polnoe sobranie stikhotvorenii* (Moscow-Leningrad, 1934), 791–92.

3. B. N. Chicherin, *Vospominaniia. Moskva sorokovykh godov* (Moscow, 1929), 3–4.

4. A partial list of such artists would include Alexander Turgenev, Pyotr Chaadaev, Alexander Herzen, Alexei Khomiakov, Konstantin and Ivan Aksakov, Vitalii Granovskii, Mikhail Pogodin, Stepan Shevyrev, Afanasy Fet, and Yakov Petrovich Polonskii, and foreign visitors such as Franz Liszt and Alexander von Humboldt. See Munir Sendich, "Moscow Literary Salons: Thursdays at Karolina Pavlova's," *Die Welt der Slaven* 17, no. 2 (1973): 341–57.

5. I. N. Pavlov, "Iz moikh vospominanii," *Russkoe obozrenie*, no. 4 (1896): 889.

6. A. S. Khomiakov, *Polnoe sobranie sochinenii* (Moscow, 1904), 7:102. This is in a letter from Khomiakov's wife, Ekaterina, to Iazykov, who was her brother.

7. N. Kovarskii, "Introduction to Karolina Pavlova," *Polnoe sobranie sochinenii* (Leningrad, 1939), vi–vii.

8. I. I. Panaev, *Literaturnye vospominaniia* (Leningrad, 1928), 288–89.

9. D. V. Grigorovich, *Literaturnye vospominaniia* (Leningrad, 1928), 193.

10. A letter of January 23, 1860, published in *I. S. Aksakov v ego pis'makh* (Moscow, 1892), 3:353.

11. Quoted in Boris Rapgof, *K. Pavlova, Materialy dlia izucheniia zhizni i tvorchestva* (P., 1916), 18–19.

12. Letter of October 12, 1854, quoted in Karolina Pavlova, *Sobranie sochinenii*, ed. V. Briusov (Moscow, 1915), 2:330–32.

13. Rapgof, 73. One critic, in a recent biography of her husband, claims that Pavlova led a life of luxury abroad (V. P. Vil'chinskii, *N. F. Pavlov*, Leningrad, 1970, 101). Quite the opposite is true, however. Nearly all of her unpublished letters of the time admit to financial as well as moral distress. See, for example, two letters in the Manuscript Division of the Saltykov-Shchedrin Library, Fond 852, N. 784; and Fond 66, N. 1, 46–47. The latter reads: "Je suis hors d'état d'agir, incapable même de vouloir, et horriblement seule."

14. A. K. Tolstoi, *Sobranie sochinenii*, 4:329, 347, and passim.

15. See B. Ya. Bukhshtab, ed., *Poety 1840-1850-kh godov* (Moscow-Leningrad, 1962), 35.

16. V. Khodasevich, "Odna iz zabytykh," *Novaia zhizn'*, (1916), 3:198.

17. Pavlova, *Sobranie sochinenii*, 303.

18. Ibid., 383. This story now can be read in English in *An Anthology of Russian Women's Writing 1777–1992*, edited by Catriona Kelly (Oxford, 1994), 30–70. For an excellent analysis, see Diana Greene, "Karolina Pavlova's 'At the Tea Table' and the Politics of Class and Gender," *Russian Review* (April, 1994), 271–84, and her *Reinventing Romantic Poetry: Russian Women Poets of the Mid-Nineteenth Century* (Madison: University of Wisconsin Press, 2004).

19. Madame de Genlis, *Nouveaux contes moraux et nouvelles historiques* (Paris, 1804), 3:61–62.

20. Anonymous, "Dvoinaia zhizn'. Ocherk K. Pavlovoi," *Sovremennik*, vol. 7, no. 3 (1848), 47.

21. "Dvoinai zhizn' ", 52–53.

A DOUBLE LIFE

DEDICATION

To you the offering of this thought,
The greeting of my poetry,
To you this work of solitude,
O slaves of din and vanity.
In silence did my sad sigh name
You Cecilys unmet by me,
All of you Psyches without wings,
Mute sisters of my soul!
God grant you, unknown family,
One sacred dream mid sinful lies,
In the prison of this narrow life
Just one brief burst of that other life.

September 1846

Our life is twofold; Sleep hath its own world,
A boundary between the things misnamed
Death and existence.

Byron

01

"**B**ut are they rich?"

"I think so; the estate is sizable. They live well enough. Besides the usual Saturdays, they give several balls during the winter; he himself doesn't enter into things; his wife handles everything; *c'est une femme de tête*."

"What's the daughter like?"

"Nothing special! Good-looking enough and not stupid, they say, but who is stupid nowadays? Anyway, I've never discussed anything with her except the weather and dances, but she must have a touch of her father's German blood. I can't stand all these Germans and half-Germans."

"A good match?"

"No! There's a younger brother."

"What do people do there on Saturdays?"

"Well, they mostly talk. Not too many people there. You'll see."

"Oh, I'm so fed up with conversations! You can't escape from them."

The carriage stopped at the entrance of a large house on Tverskoi Boulevard.

2 \\ A Double Life

"Here we are," said one of the two young men who were sitting in it, and both got out and ran up the wrought-iron staircase. In the vestibule, they made sure with a glance that their German-tailored clothing was fitted just right; they entered, bowed to their hostess, and looked around.

In the elegant drawing room were about thirty people. Some were talking among themselves in low tones, some were listening, others passing through; but it seemed as if all of them were weighed down by a sense of duty, evidently quite onerous, and it seemed that they all found amusing themselves a bit boring. There were no loud voices or arguments, nor any cigars either. This was a drawing room completely *comme il faut*; even the ladies did not smoke.

Not far from the door sat the hostess on one of those nondescript pieces of furniture that fills our rooms these days. In another corner stood a tea table. Nearby, some exceedingly nice young girls were whispering among themselves. A bit farther away, next to a large bronze clock on which it had just struck half past ten, a very noteworthy and graceful woman, submerged (so to speak) in a huge velvet armchair, was conversing with three young men sitting near her. They were talking about someone.

"He died this morning," one of them said.

"Nothing to mourn about," answered his lovely neighbor, looking at him in the most charming way.

"Well," said one youth, smiling, "he was not so young anymore but very handsome; he was wicked but clever."

"He was simply unbearable," said the lady, "and I never liked his looks; there was something angry about them."

"Who has died?" softly asked a shapely, pale, dark-haired girl of eighteen, going up to the tea table and bowing to one of the ladies near it. "Who has died, Olga?"

"I don't know," Olga replied.

The dark-haired girl sat down at the table and started to pour tea.

The graceful lady in the velvet armchair continued her clever conversation with the three young men. Judging by that conversation, it was limp and banal enough, but to judge by the expressions, the smiles and glances of the people talking, it was extremely lively and sophisticated.

"Who is that, Cécile?" Olga whispered to the young girl pouring tea.

Cecily looked up.

"The man who came in with Ilichev? I forget his name. It's the first time he's ever come to our house. It seems he's a poet."

Olga gave a haughty pout and turned her head toward the other side of the room. Two more men appeared. One of them led the other to the hostess, Vera Vladimirovna von Lindenborn, and introduced him. She greeted them most pleasantly.

"I am truly glad to be able to meet you at last. I hope that some time you will give us the pleasure of hearing you read your work."

Vera Vladimirovna was not only a highly educated woman who entertained poets and artists, but also a woman of tact. She did not wish to put her visitor's talent to use the very first time.

In the opposite corner of the drawing room, a distinguished man with graying hair barely perceptible in the candlelight, with a certain artificial carelessness in his dress and pretensions to profundity and perspicacity, went up to a young dandy leaning toward the window, whose eccentric hairstyle and spotless gloves were silhouetted very effectively against the heavy, cherry-colored curtain that fell to the parquet floors and set off his waistcoat, of the latest Parisian cut. He did not even contemplate having any other affectation.

"Look at the group near the tea table," the distinguished man said to him. "Shall I tell you what is going on there? Sophia Strenetskaia is wondering where she can find a magnanimous bridegroom who will rescue the family from inevitable poverty and clear their debts to the Board of Guardians. Olga Valitskaia is out of sorts because Prince Victor has not come. Princess Alina is laughing so hard in vain; the victorious Uhlan won't leave her cousin alone today, and the latter is using him to infuriate a certain other gentleman in the room. Amusing, isn't it?"

"You're a terrible man!" the young dandy respectfully answered, twirling his whiskers.

The terrible man smiled condescendingly.

In the mature ladies' circle, the conversation was more innocent.

"Will you be moving to the Park soon?" Vera Vladimirovna was asked by a tall, important-looking lady sitting next to her, who until then had observed a strict silence.[1]

"In about two weeks, at the beginning of June," she answered. "It seems the bad weather has passed. Will you be there too?"

"Yes, I love it. At least there you can spend the summer in good society, not like in the country, where you have to get along with God knows what kind of neighbors."

---

1. The "Park" referred to was an open, landscaped area within the city limits, with high-end dachas for rent during the summer months. Petrovsky Park is northwest of central Moscow. In Pavlova's time, it had become a fashionable location for dachas by the royal edict of 1836.

"I agree completely," said another well-dressed lady of forty, who wore roses in her hair and short sleeves as a kind of antidote against old age. "I am terribly glad to have escaped the district of Ryazan. My husband was absolutely set on taking me there for the summer, but thanks to my brother's wedding, I'm lucky enough to end up in Petersburg instead of Ryazan. Even here in Moscow, I'm feeling a little stifled."

"You're an enemy of Moscow," remarked Vera Vladimirovna.

"Why? I only share the opinion of Napoleon and think that, except for two or three salons such as this one, Moscow is a large village. And I admit I'm not devoted to villages."

Meanwhile, the pouring of tea ceased, and Cecily and the young girls went out on the wide balcony. It was a magnificent May night, full of stars. The lindens growing green in front of the balcony rustled so softly, so harmoniously sadly, so mysteriously that it seemed as if they were growing not on the Tverskoi Boulevard, but in the free expanse of virgin nature. Cecily leaned on the iron railing and became lost in thought about heaven knows what.

Her friends were laughing among themselves. One, a lively blonde girl, with her back to the railing, looked through a lorgnette at the drawing room and made her remarks in a semiwhisper. She was obliged to make fun of people because she had the reputation of being very witty.

"I think," she said, "that that blue dress will soon get a medal, it's done such long service."

The girls almost burst out laughing.

One of them asked, "Doesn't my brother's uniform become him?"

"Not at all," said the blonde. "A man in a uniform should be swarthy and dark-haired, like Chatsky,[2] for example. Don't you agree, Cecily, that Chatsky is very handsome?"

"Not in my opinion," Cecily answered. "His features are too sharp. I like a man to have a modest appearance, and even an almost feminine shyness."

"Where is Dmitry Ivachinsky?" the blonde suddenly asked her.

"He's visiting his father in the country," said Cecily in a voice that showed she was blushing.

"When is he coming back?" the blonde continued with a meaningful smile.

"How should I know?" Cecily turned and went into the drawing room again.

Some mothers were already looking for their daughters, to take them home. Vera Vladimirovna came up to Cecily.

"Time to sleep, Cécile," she said. "You know that doctor's orders are for you to go to bed early, and it's already almost midnight. Go on, my dear, people will understand." She made the sign of the cross over her, and Cecily went out, walked past a long series of rooms lighted and dark, turned into a barely lit corridor, and went into her own room.

There, everything was peaceful and silent. In the adjoining room, her old Englishwoman had already been in a deep sleep for two hours.

As is well known, a young lady of the highest circles cannot exist without an Englishwoman. In our society, we do not speak English, our ladies generally read English novels in French translations, and

---

2. The dashing hero of Alexander Griboedov's verse play *Woe from Wit* (1825).

Shakespeare and Byron are completely off-limits, but if your six-year-old daughter speaks anything but English, she is badly educated. It often follows that the mother, not as well educated as her daughter, has trouble talking to her, but this inconvenience is of slight importance. A child needs an English nurse more than a mother.

Cecily called to the maid and began to undress slowly and pensively. She was thinking that most likely the summer would be pleasant, that the summerhouse would be fun, that soon Dmitry Ivachinsky would return and that they would take walks together and dance and go horseback riding. But at the same time, in the midst of these happy thoughts, a strange and inexplicable one kept breaking through—a heavy and persistent feeling, as if she were being made to guess a riddle, find a word, remember a name and was not able to . . . Finally, she lay down, the maid went out carrying the candle, and everything grew quiet. In the cozy, soundless room, the small lamp flickered in front of the icon of the Savior.

The clock on the small column between the windows struck half past twelve with one resounding stroke in the silence. Cecily's gaze wandered lazily around the bedroom; the peaceful icon in its brilliant setting came and went before her eyes; then drowsiness closed them . . . but the question in her soul just would not fall asleep . . . how had it been? . . . who? . . . and where? . . .

The heavenly vault shone with stars . . .
The mist was dispelled . . . a fragrance wafted in . . .
Is this a chamber, airy and wondrous?
Is this a rich and moonlit garden?
How clear is the sleepless lament of the fountain!
How familiar to her the bounds of the unknown!

Bowing to her with a fragrant caress,
All around the timid flowers shine.
The moon is silent in the depths of air,
Like a clear pearl in the sea's boundlessness;
A hollow answer sounds in the leaves far off,
Like a whispering lyre, and is borne into the distance.
And the midnight radiance of all the worlds,
And all the sighs, gliding through silence,
And all the fragrant breaths of spring
Melt into a single harmony.

What secret knowledge
Troubles her young soul?
Whom does she wait for,
Whose arrival does she sense?
Over whom have sycamores bowed down?
What will shine bright in that darkness?—
Commanding gaze,
Victorious brow.
She remembers what never was,
Recognizes what she has never met.
He is reflected in the mirror of her thoughts
Like the light of a star in a mirror of water.
He stands, powerful and stern,
Stands unmoving and silent;
He looks into her eyes with his eyes,
Looks into her soul with his soul,
What reproach of guilt, of error,
Brings a frown to that brow?

On that unsmiling countenance
What a melancholy love!
What lay so heavy on the young girl's heart
Like an inescapable sentence? . . .
She walks—walks against her will
Across distances ever more silent
To where, powerful and despondent
That glance shines, like a summons.
And she stood before the unknown force,
Bowing a submissive head.
And from his lips there came a word
Sadder than the song of far-off streams;
It seemed as if a gentle kiss
Had touched her youthful brow.

02

O n Sunday morning, Cecily stood before her mirror and dressed hurriedly, for ten o'clock had already struck. The maid came in.

"Your mother asked me to see if you will be ready soon, Miss."

"Tell her I'm coming right away."

"Your mother asked me to beg you to dress up a little more and to wear your white hat. After mass, they wish to go visiting."

"All right."

She put on her white hat and went to her mother.

A few minutes later, they were both sitting in the best carriage, and the enormous lackey, slamming the doors, called out loudly, "To Sheremetevskaya!"

With a pious prayer, Vera Vladimirovna set out with Cecily, at first to visit an elderly aunt, where it was necessary to sit through an hour, out of respect for the years and estate of the childless old lady. Everything there was old-fashioned: a dirty vestibule, toy dogs, lackeys in nankeen frock-coats, and barefoot maids. Everything was united in a surprisingly harmonious way, internally and externally, body and soul. When the set hour had somehow gone by, mother and daughter again were seated in their carriage and went farther, to another part of town, another century, another world, where there were vestibules with carpets, important-looking stewards, and servants wearing gloves.

With the topographical knowledge of ladies, they rode far and wide in Moscow—from Miasnitskaya Street to the Arbat, from the Arbat to the Petrovka—and finally to the study of Madame Valitskaia, the mother of Cecily's best friend, Olga Alexeevna.

Madame Valitskaia, a very rich woman, a woman extremely stern in all her opinions and judgments, fully merited the respect of high society, for which neither the future nor the past exists. Zealously she paid her debt to virtue and morality—all the more so because she had set about this a little late, without ever thinking for the better half of her life that there would be such a price, but then, becoming convinced that it was unavoidable, she—one must do her justice—endeavored with an improbable commitment to pay the aforementioned debt and all interest that had accrued.

Most likely, there is no person so inexperienced as to be surprised that Vera Vladimirovna, in spite of her customary virtuousness and her implacable rules of conduct, was on friendly terms with Madame Valitskaia. Who would think of worrying about the past youth of a woman who for ages had led the most decorous life and, moreover, who received the best society, gave magnificent balls, and was always ready to do a favor for her friends? Society, with all its strictness, is sometimes kind-hearted: depending on the circumstances, it looks with such Christian forgiveness upon powerful people, upon prominent and wealthy women! And besides, in the aristocratic educated world, everything is angled so smoothly, the sharp edges so blunted, and each monstrous and rotten affair called by such decent language that every shameful thing is glossed over in such fine circumstances, effortlessly and quietly. If some ignoramus in some drawing room recalled Madame Valitskaia's past adventures, he would not have found anyone who knew anything about them, and he would have been told it was a calumny that was invented about an intelligent and sweet woman who in her youth perhaps had been just a bit flighty. In general, in society gatherings they don't like to speak about vice, probably for the same reason that in olden times, people didn't like to refer to the devil, fearing his presence.

And so Madame Valitskaia in the midst of such civilized company was, as they say in that foreign language, *parfaitement bien posée*. Vera Vladimirovna found particular profit in this friendship. The tone of Madame Valitskaia's drawing room satisfied her wishes fully. She knew that nowhere would she find a more strict and careful circle of friends; that nowhere would Cecily be safer; that here, she would not hear a single light-minded word or remark. And experience showed to what extent Vera Vladimirovna was right, because, as the French proverb goes, in the house of a hanged man, they don't talk about rope—so at Natalia Afanasevna Valitskaia's, they didn't even talk about thread.

When she found out about Cecily's arrival, Olga Valitskaia went hurriedly into her mother's room. The young girls, although they had parted only the evening before, embraced as if they had been separated for a year, sat on the sofa in the corner, whispered together for a few minutes, and then jumped up again.

"*Maman*," said Olga, "we're going to my room." She slipped through the door with Cecily.

Vera Vladimirovna looked after them:

"How pretty Olga has become!" she remarked.

"Cécile is twice as pretty," answered Madame Valitskaia, "but you have to look after her health more carefully; she is still a bit upset. You are right not to take her to Anna Sergeevna's ball today."

"Yes, it's wiser. I won't go either, although yesterday the Princess begged me to. What a lovely and praiseworthy woman!"

"An unusually good mother," said Madame Valitskaia.

"And a happy mother," added Vera Vladimirovna, "Prince Victor is a remarkable young man."

Madame Valitskaia's face assumed a solemn expression, and she looked down modestly, saying, "Unfortunately, one cannot fully approve his conduct."

"Of course," answered Vera Vladimirovna in a voice resonant with Madame Valitskaia's moral intonation, "but we must not judge him too harshly. Where can one find a young man who would not more or less deserve the same reproach? And then, time erases everything, and a virtuous wife can completely reform a flighty husband."

Madame Valitskaia cast a momentary glance at her friend that said "Aha," and barely perceptibly bit her lips.

"I thought of not going to that ball myself," she said, "but Olga begged me to. She very much wants to see the young people it's being given for. What a child she is! She dances and amuses herself like a ten-year-old. I don't mind in the least. You know I completely share your views on upbringing and have to admit that you couldn't apply them with more success. Cécile is the best proof of their correctness."

Vera Vladimirovna began to play with her lorgnette with self-satisfied modesty.

"Yes, I have to admit that my efforts have not failed. Cécile is exactly what I wanted to make of her. Every kind of daydreaming is foreign to her. I knew how to make reason important to her, and she will never occupy herself with empty infatuations; but naturally I haven't, so to speak, taken my eyes off her."

"The first obligation of a mother," remarked Madame Valitskaia. "We should always be able to read into the souls of our daughters, in order to foresee any harmful influences and keep them safe in all their childlike innocence."

While the mothers were conversing thus in the study, their daughters were carrying on a completely different kind of conversation in Olga's room. The elderly Englishwoman was also there, but all her attention was turned to some endless quilt she had been working on from time immemorial. Besides, like all our Englishwomen, she understood scarcely more than twenty Russian words; and so Olga, sitting next to her friend, immediately began speaking Russian.

"So you won't be taken to the Princess's ball tonight?"

"No, *maman* says that I'm too tired and have to take care of myself."

"Well, you do look quite pale today; what's the matter?"

"My head aches; I slept badly. Imagine, Olga, I had a dream about the man they were talking about yesterday at our house, the one who had died that morning."

"God protect you! Who is it?"

"I don't know myself; remember at the tea table, they were talking about someone?"

"You are always having dreams about nonsense and various horrible things. What a shame that you're not going to the ball! It's being given for the young people, and they say it will be wonderful. The daughter's gown comes from Paris. Do you want to see my dress?"

Without waiting for an answer, Olga rang the bell.

"Masha! Bring out my dress."

The maid carried in a lovely, airy dress with a waist decorated with marvelous ribbons, a double skirt, one falling on top of the other like a rosy mist—an exquisite dress! Cecily looked at it and fully appreciated its worth.

"Who made it? Madame André?"

"Yes, she agreed to against her will; eleven dresses have been ordered from her for tonight. I was scared to death she wouldn't do it. How disappointing you aren't going! I am engaged for nearly every dance; I've promised the mazurka to Prince Victor."

"Is Prince Victor going to Petersburg?" asked Cecily in a semiwhisper.

Olga lowered her eyes and replied even more quietly:

"I don't know; maybe he'll go."

"You mean if you wish it?"

"No, darling," Olga whispered, clasping her friend's hand, "not yet. God knows what will happen. Only, for God's sake, don't tell anyone. *Maman* has strictly forbidden me to say a word about it, especially to you. You know she thinks you want to marry Prince Victor yourself. She doesn't know you're thinking about someone else."

Cecily smiled, and in a few minutes, the maid Masha announced: "Cecily Alexandrovna! Your mother has sent for you; she wants to leave right away."

Both friends ran downstairs. Vera Vladimirovna was already standing with Madame Valitskaia in the hall, ready to set out for home. The old friends shook hands, and the young ones embraced three times and finally parted.

On the staircase of her house, Vera Vladimirovna met her nephew.

"Hello, Serge! Where are you going?"

"I dropped in to ask how you are, *ma tante*, and now I'm off to Ilichev's. I'm having dinner with him at Chevalier's."

"Well, I don't want to keep you. Goodbye, my friend."

She went up several steps and stopped again. "A propos, Serge, listen!"

"What is it, *ma tante*?"

"You probably know that young man. What's his name? The one Ilichev introduced me to yesterday, the writer."

"Yes, I know, *ma tante*."

"Do me a favor—bring him to me next Saturday so that he can read us something. Yesterday evening was not a success for some reason, and next Saturday will be the last one, so I have to fill it up with something or other. It's a real penance!"

"All right, *ma tante*, I'll get the writer for you."

"Please don't forget."

"For heaven's sake!"

The nephew ran downstairs; the aunt went to her room.

Nearly all of Vera Vladimirovna's acquaintances were at the ball that day, so she spent a very quiet evening at home. Still, two old ladies and one no longer young dropped in. They and their hostess made a foursome for a game of preference, the best way to pass the time in such circumstances. Vera Vladimirovna's husband—he was generally referred to as "the husband of Vera Vladimirovna," and once when a stranger asked him with whom he had the pleasure of speaking, he introduced himself thus—Vera Vladimirovna's husband—was, as always, at his club.

Cecily had a bad headache toward evening. After pouring the tea, she asked permission to go to bed.

"Of course, my dear," said her mother, "but shouldn't we send for the doctor?"

"No, *maman*, it's nothing. By tomorrow, I'll be fine."

She kissed her mother's hand, went to her room, and lay down.

An unusual weariness, probably the result of her morning visits, took hold of her. She didn't know why, but her heart felt heavy. She lay down for a long time without sleeping, her eyes closed. Tiredness weighed her down more and more. Her thoughts grew still; sleep flew in to her. She forgot everything, but through that forgetfulness, some indistinct memory melted and grew clear in the depths of her soul. It seemed as if someone spread a misty veil over her head, and she let herself down softly, softly, softly—suddenly, a shiver ran through her body:

As if a miracle had been accomplished . . .
"As you were yesterday, you're here with me again!"
"I'm here with you, and will be faithful to you!
I've waited for you, I whom you called for, yours."

"Who are you?"
 "I am that which you sought
In the radiance of starry heights.
I am your sadness in the tumult of a ball,
I am the secret of your dream
That you could not reach with reason,
That you have understood with your heart.
Rushing into a world rich with thought,
Did you not go beyond its limits?

Weren't you filled with the unknown,
Didn't you look into the distance?
Not knowing loss, still
Didn't you miss something all the same?"

They sit in the moonlight,
And a silver stream sings to them.
"Yes, it's you! You have come from the grave, alive!
Is it possible, or am I dreaming?"

"How may a creature of the earth know
What is impossible or possible?
Perhaps everything there was false,
Perhaps only here you are awake.

That prisoner of society's world,
That sacrifice to vanity,
The blind slave of custom,
That small-souled being isn't you.

They have fettered you from childhood,
Have swaddled your free mind,
Deprived you of your eternal inheritance,
Freedom of feeling and the kingdom of thought.

And under the iron yoke of the age
Joyful impulses were silenced in your heart,
But in the sinful human body
God's spirit has remained alive.

So only for a fleeting moment
You take wing with a free soul.
In life's deadness there is an incorporeal region
In the midst of that world, another world.

You will understand inspiration's secret,
You will live the soul's life fully.
What the genius learns in waking
You will learn, my child, in sleep.

Yet you will forget what you have learned.
I will not poison your days,
I will not lift the veil
From your eyes, in that land of the blind.

And there my word will fall silent
The traces of my love will disappear;
Mid people's talk you will remember
Me like an empty dream.

But the spirit of silence will enter,
The world will fall asleep like a quiet house,
And, flaming with prayer,
The stars will stand before their creator.

And I will come to you unknown,
In the quiet, in a marvelous dream;
With the mysterious force of a kiss
I will lift the shackles from your soul,

So that the holy song may sound,
And incense rise,
And the divine service flame up
Again in you, the silent temple."

03

Vera Vladimirovna's final Saturday was a huge success: the coveted poet appeared. The company that evening consisted of the most select lovers of literature, both men and women. These days, it is not at all difficult to get such a group together since literature is extremely respected, and ladies especially have been devoting such attention to it for some time that only by hardly noticeable signs is it possible to guess that, in fact, they play no active part in it.

And so the poet appeared: a shy, rather awkward young man, his gloves not quite fresh. He entered with some feelings of timid pride into the well-lighted and enlightened drawing room where so many important persons, so many beautiful women, had gathered to hear him. But right now, they all had something else on their minds: Vera Vladimirovna's nephew had unexpectedly brought her a traveler just arrived in Moscow, a Spanish count, terribly interesting, a swarthy proud Carlist with sparkling eyes. Naturally he became the object of general attention, the focus of all female glances, and the focus of the drawing room. All the ladies present were busy trying with fervent effort to please the new arrival, to ingratiate themselves with the foreign visitor by that well-known, incurable hospitality that is sometimes so fond and jealous that it becomes a bit indecent and often makes us appear comical and our foreign guests arrogant. The poor man of letters stood in a corner, completely unnoticed. But what is so surprising in the fact that no one so much as glanced at him in such an unforeseen event? For Moscow ladies, men of letters are nothing unusual, but a Spanish count is still something of a novelty.

But after a couple of hours, the count left, and then the hostess turned her attention to the poet. She went up to him and told him in a very nice way about her own and everyone else's impatience for and expectation of the recital he had promised. Then she seated him by a table with the audience around him, herself magnanimously occupying the most prominent place nearest him, where it would be impossible either to whisper or to yawn. The poor young man was a bit troubled and began to turn the pages of his notebook, not knowing what to select from it. Everything he did made it clear that it was the first time that he was preparing to deal with this class of people, who are separated from the rest of humanity and compose that haughty fashionable "world," as it is so naively called, for which no other world exists in the Lord's universe.

Because Cecily and other young ladies were there, the recital had to be completely moral and blameless, and the timid poet, after some hesitation, finally decided to read his unpublished translation of Schiller's "Bell." He coughed and said in a modest voice, "The Song of the Bell." A minute's silence followed, a few graceful heads leaned forward, some rosy lips smiled sweetly, some lovely listeners fixed affable looks upon the young poet while making a mental note that this was a very long piece. Emboldened by such flattering attention, the young man began to read, at first in a soft voice, then in a louder and livelier one. He was so young and inexperienced that he read his verse before that aristocratic society with the same passion with which he spoke them alone to himself in his modest room. He was so tempered in the flame of poetry that he did not sense the worldly coldness of all these people. He placed before them a series of magically changing views: a peaceful childhood, a stormy youth and the ecstasy of love, quiet happiness, grief come from heaven, the flame of fire, the gloom of devastation and a mother's death, and then, in the distance, meadows in the light of evening with the herds slowly returning, the night quietly falling, healing calm and sudden, terrible restlessness, the joys of life and the sorrows, ringing forth in the prayerful, fateful sound of the bell, and finally, from his burning lips, the last inspired words flew:

And henceforth may this be
Its destiny
Amid the heavens' expanse
Carried high above Earth,
May it float, near to thunder
And approach the world of stars.
May its holy voice come from on high
Like all the constellation's choir
May it praise the universe-creator
And bring along a generous year.
May it proclaim with bronze tongue
Only that which is sacred and omnipotent;
May the wing of time beat within it
Every hour as it goes by.

And may it be the word of fate,
Standing unconsciously above all,
May it herald from afar
The game of Earth's reality,
And startling us from on high
With powerful sounds,
May it teach us that all is not eternal,
That all things earthly will pass.

The notebook fell from his hands. He fell silent.

"*C'est délicieux! C'est charmant!*" whispered a few voices.

Vera Vladimirovna repeated, with emotion, "*C'est charmant!*" and thanked the poet for the pleasure he had given them.

"How fine that was," said Cecily into Olga's ear.

"Very good," Olga replied, looking intently at someone through her lorgnette.

A short silence ensued.

"Yes," said a short, sweetly smiling little man of about fifty, "that thought about time is a very felicitous one, but a bit drawn out in the German manner. With what strength and compression Jean-Baptiste Rousseau managed to express it in two lines:

Le temps, cette image mobile
De l'immobile Eternité."

One lady among the charming neighbors of the man of letters leaned close to him and asked sympathetically, "How long did this marvelous translation take you?"

"I don't know," answered the poor, confused young man.

She turned away with a barely perceptible smile.

"That is really good poetry," said a lean, serious man, Prince Some-body, quietly sitting in a large armchair, "but it's . . ." (he stopped for a moment, took a pinch of snuff, stretched his right leg over his left, and continued) "but it's not very contemporary poetry. We are not content any more with empty dreaming; we demand action. In our century, a poet should labor alongside this hardworking generation; poetry should be useful; it should hold vice up to shame or set a crown on virtue."

Vera Vladimirovna stood up for Schiller.

"Permit me, Prince," she remarked, "it seems to me that you are not quite right about the poem; there is much that is morally edify-ing and truly useful in it."

"Yes," interrupted the prince, inflamed by his own eloquence, "but it is all somehow not alive enough, not expressive enough. We want to see the point of a poem clearly. Understand this," he contin-ued, turning to the poet, "your noble calling is more important now than ever, morally higher. Write poetry against cold-hearted egotists, against the debauches of flighty young people, stir the conscience of the evildoer, and then you will be a contemporary poet. We recog-nize only what is useful to mankind."

The poor young poet thought for a moment, perhaps, that to feel and to reason, to love and to pray—this too might be somewhat use-ful for humanity; but he was silent.

Vera Vladimirovna wanted to ask him to read another poem, but looking around, she saw that everyone seemed a bit wearied by the delights of poetry. Besides, it was already pretty late, and her eve-ning could end satisfactorily without the aid of any new artistic admixture. And indeed, this society of literary dilettantes gradually dispersed, looking quite content, and their praises were even heard on the stairway:

"A young man with talent."

"And the Spaniard will be at my house tomorrow."

"He's very interesting."

"Marvelous eyes."

"What a pleasant evening!"

"Especially since it's over," a haughty youth added in passing, setting his hat to perch smartly on his brow.

An hour after the reading, the rich drawing room was empty, and Cecily was sitting at her dressing table, putting her heavy black hair up in curls for the night.

She felt somehow strange and awkward. Involuntarily, she remembered and repeated some of the lines she had heard. Sharply delineated visions flashed by her again, and all of this went quite beyond the customary bounds of her thoughts.

Cecily had been educated in the fear of God and society; the Lord's Commandments and the laws of propriety carried equal weight with her. To destroy either, even in thought, seemed to her equally impossible and inconceivable. And although, as we have seen, Vera Vladimirovna greatly respected and loved poetry, she still considered it improper for a young girl to spend too much of her time on it. She quite justly feared any development of imagination and inspiration, those eternal enemies of propriety. She molded the spiritual gifts of her daughter so carefully that Cecily, instead of dreaming of the Marquis Poza, of Egmont, of Lara and the like, could only dream of a splendid ball, a new gown, and the outdoor fete on the first of May.

Vera Vladimirovna was, as we have seen, very proud of her daughter's successful upbringing, especially perhaps because it had been accomplished not without difficulty, because it took time and skill to destroy in her soul its innate thirst for delight and enthusiasm. Be that as it may, Cecily, prepared for high society, having memorized all its requirements and statutes, could never commit the slightest peccadillo, the most barely noticeable fault against them, could never forget herself for a moment, raise her voice half a tone, jump from a chair, enjoy a conversation with a man to the point where she might talk to him ten minutes longer than was proper or look to the right when she was supposed to look to the left. Now, at eighteen, she was so used to wearing her mind in a corset that she felt it no more than she did the silk undergarment that she took off only at night. She had talents, of course, but measured ones, decorous ones, *les talents de société*, as the language of society so aptly calls them. She sang very nicely and sketched very nicely as well. Poetry, as we have said earlier, was known to her mostly by hearsay, as something wild and incompatible with a respectable life. She knew that there were even women poets, but this was always presented to her as the most pitiable, abnormal condition, as a disastrous and dangerous illness.

But now she was thinking involuntarily about that strange ability of the soul. Unconsciously, there awakened in her a new and obscure sympathy for that harmony of verse, for those melodious thoughts, those improper delights, and this unexpected sympathy almost frightened her. Her reason told her that after all, this was empty and unnecessary nonsense that shouldn't occupy her for long. And thinking this, she laid her graceful head on the pillow and was alone in the silence of the night. But no, through her drowsiness, rhyme sounded in her again; she heard poetry and, half asleep, she suddenly thought that she too could speak in song . . . and drowsily smiled at the absurdity of it. But a persistent song hummed and sounded and lulled her. She heard it more clearly all the time, and its harmonies and inspired words appeared more and more real to her. It seemed as if waves were lifting her ... she was in a small boat ... carrying her far away ... and then she glimpsed the shore; the moon came up ...

The river flows and whispering goes
  The river's stream.
A boat is carried past, untiring
  Down the river.

A melody slips through the silence
  To meet a maiden
Like a far-off echo, like a musical
  Chord a wave makes.

And powerful, along with the wave
  Thoughts sing in her;
With a mighty sound there soars at night
  The flight of dreams,

  Of dreams despondent and tense,
  Everything the mind has saved in vain.
  Of the sad and godless loss
  Of greatest happiness and strength.
  Of false worldly barriers,
  Of intrigues of worldly judges,
  Of everything murdered without mercy,
  Of everything that has perished without trace.

The river flows, and whispering goes
   The river's stream.
And with the maiden, untiring,
   The boat slips past.

It floats far at the current's will
   And the choir of stars
Far-shining, with reproachful beam,
   Meets her glance.

The Milky Way leads to an endless world
   Far above her
And a heartfelt sigh flies sadly up
   To that eternity.

"Perhaps with the passing years
A better age will come:
Mankind will not always be
A sacrifice to worldly sin!
Maybe days of hope
Of blessedness are near,
And holy yearnings once again
Will start up in the soul.
But why meet these reproaches,
Why perish vainly in the shadows,
Prophets without usefulness,
Whom God sends to Earth today?
You drink to the dregs in vain
The bitter cup of life;

Your faith is alien to men,
They do not need your song."

And past, past untiring
  The boat slips through;
The river flows and loudly goes
  The river's stream.

And all the waves sing, blending
  Their sonorous voices;
And an alien distance, a mute region
  Answers back.

The wind flying in the drowsing shade
  Through the waters' foam,
Through the roar, carries forth
  A mighty answer.

And on they go amid upheavals
  Hurling their loud verses to the world;
  To them, song is more than human striving,
  Dreams are more necessary than worldly gifts.
  Their conviction has no answer,
  Their inspiration no reward.
  But, inaccessible to worldly power,
  They sing. They do not create
  For the empty joys of the masses—
  For whom, in vain, life fills with miracles
  The myriads of stars shine forth,

And the sun gleams in the heavens—
But so that people, sensing this mystery,
Will not be able to reject it;
So that the poet's alleluia
Will rise above Earth's murmur:
Because for the universe this is
An inexhaustible blessing,
For holy gifts are everywhere
Where there is someone to understand them.
For every creature of the world
Must, fulfilling its existence,
Contribute its own fragrance,
Shine with its own light through the darkness.
Not in vain in the distant desert
The sun for years has scorched the palm,
If one day, tortured by the heat,
Even one brow should find repose;
If, in the sterile scorching land,
A single traveler, deprived of strength,
Should find even an hour of peace,
And bless the palm tree's shade.

04

Several days had passed since Vera Vladimirovna had moved into one of those nice pseudo-Gothic-Chinese buildings scattered around Petrovsky Park. Here too, everything corresponded to the demands and conditions of society. Surrounding the luxurious cottage was a luxurious garden, its greenery always an excellent, a choice, or one might say an aristocratic greenery. Nowhere was there a faded leaf, a dry twig, a superfluous blade of grass; banished was everything in God's creation that was coarse, vulgar, plebeian. The very shrubbery around the house flaunted a kind of Parisian haughtiness—the very flowers planted in every available space took on a certain semblance of good form; nature made herself unnatural. In a word, everything was as it should be.

In the midst of this beautiful and artful decor, on a warm and clear June evening, some saddled horses were standing. Three of them had ladies' saddles on them and fancy grooms alongside. Around them paced and fretted five or six young dandies, both Prince Victor and Dmitry Ivachinsky, who had only recently arrived, among them. A little farther away, a large carriage and two light carriages for men were waiting, harnessed and ready. The ladies were sitting in the drawing room waiting for those who were riding and who were still getting into their riding habits. They finally appeared, and the entire party went out onto the wide porch. Cecily and Olga, more slender than usual in long riding dresses of a dark color, even more graceful in black caps almost like those the men wore, under which their thick hair tumbled out and their lively eyes shone, stopped on the iron steps, whips in hand, brave and beautiful. The restless horses were brought to them. No sooner had they placed their narrow feet in the stirrups than off they flew. They flicked the reins and were carried far ahead of the men, with that violent female daring which is so far from manly valor.

The third horsewoman was one of those precious and useful friends with whom clever society women usually provide themselves. She belonged to the countless majority of ladies who have no money, no beauty, and not even attractive minds—futile and insufficient substitutes for these two more important possessions. On the other hand, Nadezhda Ivanovna was essential to Madame Valitskaia; Nadezhda Ivanovna shared in all the merriment of that brilliant circle and, poor thing, every day, without tiring, she set her thick figure, her thirty-year-old, ordinary face, her miserable dress alongside Olga's graceful figure, fresh face, and marvelously artful clothes, and she probably did not understand herself how selfless she was being. Or maybe she did understand—how can we know? There are people who are ready to pay with the blood from their own veins in order to brush up against high society and, as it were, play a part in its amusements.

The destination of the ride was Ostankino.

The cavalcade, accompanied by the carriages, was already passing a cool, wide grove which the common folk, with their native good sense, chose for their amusements and made unquestionably their own, leaving the dusty Petrovsky Park and sandy Sokolniki to the more enlightened people. Cecily galloped forward. With childish joy, she gave herself over to the fun of riding horseback, to the attraction of this living force, this half-free will that carried her off and that she was guiding. Besides, the late afternoon was beautiful, the meadows wide, the air invigorating, the sky endlessly clear. She struck her horse with the whip and went forward at top speed. A sort of incomprehensible intoxication possessed her. She suddenly wanted to gallop away from life's imprisonment, from all dependencies, from all obligations, all necessities. She rode with shining eyes, her hair flying loose. Suddenly someone caught up with her, and someone's hand grabbed the reins of her horse and stopped it.

"Did the horse run away with you?" said Prince Victor.

Cecily came to her senses and caught her breath.

"No, I gave her free rein."

"How you frightened us," he continued, adding in a low voice, "How you frightened me!"

"I did?"

"You don't believe it?"

She smiled, straightened her hair, set her cap on her forehead, and went on with the horse at a walk. The prince stayed beside her and continued the conversation.

A few minutes later, they heard a furious galloping, and Olga flew past them with Dmitry Ivachinsky. Olga was laughing.

But in the carriage, Madame Valitskaia didn't let her lorgnette fall from her eyes for a moment and was very preoccupied with Cecily. Vera Vladimirovna was sitting next to her, with a face more contented than frightened, and assured her friend that Cecily was an excellent rider and that her horse was very trustworthy and would never run away with her. Madame Valitskaia could not convince herself of this and was so shaken that once or twice she had recourse to smelling salts.

Finally, everyone arrived safely and galloped to the entrance of the Ostankino gardens. The men jumped down and helped the women, flushed with their exertion, from their mounts. In one of the pavilions, tea, fruit, and ice cream were being prepared for everyone. Meanwhile, they set off for a walk. Cecily and Olga went on ahead, surrounded by the men. The cautious Vera Vladimirovna made sure at a glance that her obliging nephew, Serge, had fully understood a few words that she had whispered to him—that he was paying great attention to Olga, and that Prince Victor was next to Cecily. And the good mother, foreseeing all, accompanied by Nadezhda Ivanovna, followed behind the young people, very content with her strategic positionings. Madame Valitskaia went last, having taken the arm of Dmitry Ivachinsky. She walked quietly and slowly, conversing with him about the charm of the evening and the cool freshness of Ostankino Park. Imperceptibly, they lagged behind the others a little. Madame Valitskaia continued the conversation in her mild, quiet voice. (She always spoke in low tones.)

"It seems we are walking around the entire park. I'm afraid that the walk will last too long and that we will have to ride home in the twilight. What time is it now, Dmitry Andreevich? I haven't a watch."

Dmitry, who hadn't the least suspicion where that most innocent of questions, "What time is it?" can lead, took out his watch and answered simple-heartedly, "Quarter to eight."

"I don't know," continued Natalia Afanasevna, "whether I will permit Olga to go home on horseback. I'm always afraid of that ride. I just had a terrible fright seeing how Cecily's horse ran away with her."

"But Cecily Alexandrovna insists that the horse did not run away with her."

"Nonsense. I saw it myself. How is it that you didn't gallop after her immediately? She was a hair's breadth from death."

"Well, I . . . I didn't notice anything. She was ahead of me."

"That's just fine! But Prince Victor noticed right away and raced headlong to stop the horse."

Dmitry smiled faintly.

"That proves that Prince Victor is quicker than I."

Madame Valitskaia smiled a little too, replying, "That may prove something else."

A smile remained on Dmitry's face.

"I think," he said, "that Prince Victor will never be subject to the danger of falling in love."

"Why? Cecily is extremely nice. And she will be a very good match. An old aunt decided to make Cecily her only heir after the death of her son. I know that for sure. The old lady has a considerable estate, and she isn't likely to live very long. Vera Vladimirovna was telling me only yesterday about this aunt's quite ill health. Vera Vladimirovna loves her sincerely and worries and grieves about her a great deal. Poor Vera Vladimirovna! An incomparably greater misfortune threatens her. Her young son is developing the same terrible disease which, as you know, killed three children of this unhappy mother in the first years of their lives. Cecily will probably remain her only consolation."

And with this sad thought, Madame Valitskaia bowed her head and sighed, cutting short the conversation.

Dmitry Ivachinsky was a good man, even a noble man in the ordinary sense of the word, but why should a good and noble man not wish to be a rich man as well? As with the greater part of our generation, money, even a lot of money, was the most essential element of life for him. He himself had a fine fortune, but what does a fine fortune serve in our age if it only incessantly limits one's desires and makes one feel the need for wealth even more keenly and morbidly? He had liked Cecily for a long time, but he had assumed her to be dowerless, so to speak, and calculated very sensibly and correctly that if he could only scrape by (as he expressed it) on fifteen thousand a year as a bachelor, then as a married man, things would be bad for him. Besides, he was of limited intelligence; he looked only at what was pointed out to him, and now, following these indications, he saw Cecily for the first time in a different light, one extraordinarily favorable to her. Decidedly, he did not wish for the death of her brother (or even of the old aunt), but since it was totally beyond his power to save the poor boy or the good old lady, he began to consider them already in their graves. And Cecily was decidedly a very sweet, very good-looking, and very good-hearted girl who could make a husband very happy.

Thinking about all this, Dmitry walked silently alongside Madame Valitskaia, who was also silent, thinking how incredibly easy it is to manage things with certain people.

They returned to the pavilion, where the servants were waiting with tea, and settled themselves. Madame Valitskaia went up to her daughter, who was standing some distance away, seemingly in order to fix her hair, which was completely disheveled from the ride. This motherly work lasted about ten minutes, after which Olga took Cecily by the arm and went for a stroll with her around the expanse of the gardens. None of the men dared break into this friendly conversation. It was obvious that they were both speaking in a lively fashion, especially Olga. Her mother looked on from afar and was able to see that at first, Cecily looked quite serious, but that soon she grew gayer and lowered her eyes with a very nice smile. Then Natalia Afanasevna turned to the table and with great pleasure began to eat the ice cream that had been put before her some time back.

When they had eaten and walked enough, they prepared to go home. Dmitry Ivachinsky led Cecily's horse up to her and put his hand down as a step for her graceful foot to mount.

"Cecily Alexandrovna," he said in a half-whisper, straightening her long dress, "let me ride beside you. The last time you frightened me so that I completely lost control."

"You had time to come to your senses," she replied.

"Oh. When I came to my senses, you had already been saved by the chivalrous prince, and I didn't dare bother you while you were thanking him."

Cecily, starting to laugh, slightly and very gaily, glanced quickly at Dmitry and galloped away. In that half-laugh, in that half-glance was the permission he asked for, and together, they went through a green meadow, on which the twilight had already cast its shadow and the rising moon its pale light. The abandoned Prince Victor began to bestow his attentions on Olga, considering this, in all the naivete of his self-veneration, a cruel revenge for the insult that Cecily had dealt him. The horses ran faster on the road home and soon reached their destination.

At the porch, Dmitry jumped down and went to Cecily to help her dismount. She leaned forward and jumped, supporting herself on his uplifted hand, and in half a minute that protecting, firm hand clasped her soft little one as if it never wanted to let go. Cecily came hurriedly into the house, her face flushed, but no longer just from the ride.

And you, Vera Vladimirovna, at that fateful moment you were calmly getting out of the carriage. Where was your sharp eye, watchful mother? Where was your inevitable lorgnette?

It was already midnight when Cecily, having undressed, sent away the maid and, in a light peignoir, sat by the open window of her cozy room. The warm, almost still night air blew in on her face. Small clouds swept softly across the sky. There was emptiness all around. The magnificent night even took the haughty vulgarity from Petrovsky Park. Only the mysterious expanse of space was visible, only a mass of trees shone black, only the small light of peaceful dwellings glimmered somewhere. The broad-leafed maple in front of her window was rustling softly. In the distance, the watchman was walking back and forth singing. The slow Russian song sounded forth in the quiet, a song full of subdued sadness, expansive, limitless, like its country:

The Tsar orders everyone to serve;
It happened long ago to my dear one.
Everyone has been given a steed by the Tsar;
No steed was given to my dear one,
No steed was given for him to ride.
My dear friend, use me as a hostage,
Use me as a hostage, and then buy a horse.
Serve for awhile, you will finish that work;
You will train the steed. You will rescue me.
And they all came riding home,
But no news of my dear one.

The steed runs alone, and on it lies a token,
On it lies a token, a feathered cap,
My silken shawl is in this cap.
I don't miss my shawl, carried in the cap,
I miss my friend, now with another girl,
With another girl; he quarreled with me.

For a long time, Cecily sat in quiet, indefinite meditation. Finally, tired, she lay down, still listening to the despondent melody and hearing only her own thoughts and broodings. Sadly, the far-off sounds put her to sleep; joyfully, the dreams of her heart lulled her. The leaves under her window were whispering over and over . . .

A quiet hour, foggy spaces
Warmth and emptiness;
A strange rustling in the grove,
The leaves whisper like mouths.
The vale is dark and fragrant;
The heights are bright with stars.

And the fountain, sparkling in the distance,
Scatters tears without number;
It seems as if a quiet reproach
Were heard in the land.
In the heart, young happiness
Has lain down with heavy grief.

There, like spirits of the night
Shadows go in black procession.

There, stern and powerful,
The fateful visitor will appear.
His eyes stare
Into the deep and silent gloom.

And flowing with the innate
Secret complaint of the quiet,
With the sadly whispering stream,
With the murmur of forest depths—
Surfeited with longing,
Her soul's words poured forth:

"Resign yourself! Why ask in vain?
Surely we all know what is our lot?
Not in vain, Sorrow, you enter hourly
Into woman's heart as into your own home.

When was mercy ever shown to someone weak?
And who will respect their existence?
Cliffs of Leucadia, you are not the only
Preserver of some legend of sorrow!

O, voice of love and selflessness!
You will lead us to deception and to woe.
Light of ecstasy, holy revelations,
Gifts of heaven—you are useless to us.

All is vanity! High callings,
The gush of feelings and the dream of joy,

And all the struggles, sacrifices, sufferings,
Things of Earth—all these are vanity."

The sighing stopped. And like a bright vision
He stands before the helpless girl,
And looking toward the lights of the heavens,
With the sorrowful blessing of love
He placed his hand on her head.

And rolling on like mighty waves overflowing,
The echoes of her feelings and sad thoughts
Are carried along before her
But more clearly, more sternly, and more fully:

"What do you seek, young madwoman?
Look around at what concerns the world!
Dedicate your whole life to a phantom,
Put your trust in it, and find yourself an idol!

And clothe it with your reveries
And wait for happiness, stubborn child!
It will answer the soul's passion, the heart's
      outpourings
By being bored or by joking.

At times your love will be rewarded
With a distracted, hurried kiss.
You are a woman! Learn to control yourself,
Close your lips and chain your soul.

Hold back your passion, stifle its sounds,
Teach your tears not to flow.
You are a woman! Live without defenses,
Without caprice, without will, without hope.

Do not call the slaves of need, the blind sons of worry
Into your secret world, the world of your heart:
With every day, new labors await them
They have no time for happiness and love.

But you must preserve the sacred visions,
But you, in your deceived soul,
Must learn how to keep a vow of perfect faith
In the tumult of their pagan passions.

Do not try to know their fruitless freedom,
Keep your undertakings safe from theirs;
Let people hurry and be noisy,
Don't ask what all the noise is for!

Go quietly, go to the wilderness again,
To the completion of unrewarded labor;
Go once again to what was here today,
What will be here tomorrow and forever!

And at the end of the oppressive journey
Ask why there are so many wearying days,
Why the creator's orders are so stern
And why the lot of the powerless is still harder."

05

About a week after the excursion to Ostankino, at the beginning of a sultry day, Vera Vladimirovna and her daughter were drinking tea on their balcony in the shade of some sparse, dusty, grayish trees. In front of the garden, the wide, white road glistened in the sunlight in all its brightness. The wind was raising the fine sand on the road in spirals. On both sides, the elegant sidewalk boundary posts could be seen one after the other. Opposite their house stood exactly the same kind of smart house with a balcony, flower bed, saplings, and a green fence. Both women had the notion that it was very early, about ten o'clock, and while taking their breakfast, they were enjoying what they imagined was nature and the morning.

Cecily was paler and more silent than usual. She unconsciously felt something strange and awkward inside, a feeling that she could not cope with. Her soul was so highly polished, her understanding so confused, her natural talents so overorganized and mutilated by the unsparing way that she had been brought up that every problem of life perplexed and scared her. Her mother's lessons and moral teachings were about as useful to her in relation to life as are the endless commentaries of zealous scholars to Shakespeare and Dante. Once you have read them, you can no longer grasp even the clearest and simplest meaning in what the poets have written. Her morals and intellect had been improved as arbitrarily and thoroughly as the pitiful trees in the gardens of Versailles, shamelessly pruned into columns, vases, spheres, and pyramids so that they looked like anything but trees. Mothers like Vera Vladimirovna, however, most likely understand something of the possible consequences of their method because all of them are in an unbelievable hurry to get their perfected daughters off their hands and charge someone else with this dangerous responsibility that weighs down on them.

A fast-moving carriage thundered along the noisy street in front of the house and stopped by the porch.

"It's Natalia Afanasevna," Cecily said, glancing up; and Natalia Afanasevna came in with Nadezhda Ivanovna.

"Bonjour, *chère*! You weren't expecting me so early, but I'm afraid of the heat. You know, I have to cross the whole park to see you. I got up early today like country folk, *et me voilà*. What are you doing?"

"Nothing special," Vera Vladimirovna answered. "Cécile has not been quite well these past two days, but today she's already feeling better. And then today I am having a severe dizzy spell. And Olga?"

"Olga is well; she's rushing to finish her rug for our lottery. By the way, how many tickets have you distributed?"

"Only twenty. I gave eight to Sergei."

"Please try to give out the rest of them too. I still have about fifty, but today I'm giving half of them to Princess Alina. She's wonderful at distributing them. *A propos,* are you going to poor Madame Stentsova's funeral today?"

"Well, it seems I must," answered Vera Vladimirovna, "Yesterday Princess Anna Sergeevna said that even she was going. Only I don't know what I should do. I feel decidedly so unwell today that I don't even have the strength to stand throughout the whole service. I think I won't go to the church but just take my carriage with them to the cemetery, out of respect for the old mother."

"Fine. I'll do the same thing. This morning I've an awful lot of things I have to do. I won't get to the church on time, but only toward the end of the service. So we can ride together. If you like, drop by for me; I'm on your way."

"Fine. What an unexpected death!"

"Yes, the poor woman was at the princess's last evening party."

"Yes. I was talking to her there. How old was she?"

"About thirty-two, but she seemed older."

"What a pity! She was an extremely nice and kind woman. Her husband must be out of his mind."

"That husband is quite in his mind," Madame Valitskaia answered with a slight smile. "And he doesn't have too much to grieve over anyway; his happiness was not something to envy."

"Yes, so they say. But she loved him very much."

"Yes, she loved him after her own fashion, maybe too much. At least, he himself used to declare that he would have liked to be loved a bit less."

"You mean he didn't succeed?" asked Vera Vladimirovna.

"It seems not, no matter how hard he tried."

Vera Vladimirovna remembered that Cecily was present and took advantage of the convenient opportunity to plant a moral lesson.

"For all the husband's faults," she pronounced in a stern voice, "the wife is guilty. Her duty is to know how to bind him to her and make him love virtue."

Madame Valitskaia was naturally in complete agreement with this.

The conversation lasted a few minutes longer in a similar vein, and then Natalia Afanasevna stood up.

"Well, goodbye for now. I'm leaving Nadezhda Ivanovna with you. You can bring her back to me later on. *A tantôt.* And please don't be late; be at my place at two o'clock."

She left, and Nadezhda Ivanovna, as a result of her longtime habit of not being surprised that people disposed of her with such ease, as if she were an object loaned back and forth, took from her pocket a half-finished purse, also destined for the charitable lottery, and began to crochet it.

The park's appearance was changing little by little: the sidewalks were becoming more populated, the road noisier, the dust thicker and more plentiful. Carriages bowled along, dashing men galloped by on horseback, and attractive ladies walked on either side of the road to take advantage of the midday shade. Others sat on their balconies and terraces, under the shadow of broad awnings. That whole conventional, wealthy, arrogant world was coming to life.

Ordinary people were no longer visible; those who worked had gone home. All except a peasant resting under a bush, who, hearing suddenly the furious thunder of wheels or the gallop of a horse, lifted up his head a little, looked around peacefully and lay down again, wondering silently to himself.

The time for morning visits had arrived. Two or three ladies and five or six men visited Vera Vladimirovna's salon; Dmitry Ivachinsky arrived, and Prince Victor appeared as well. They began to speak again of the sudden death of Madame Stentsova and mourned the dead woman.

"She was not at all bad-looking," said Prince Victor.

"Her complexion was too dark," said Nadezhda Ivanovna.

The prince looked at her with some surprise, not having expected the unseemly retort from this living piece of furniture, and continued lazily:

"Not at all bad-looking, remarkable eyes, only terribly boring."

"Quite an empty woman," said one lady. "I could never talk to her for more than ten minutes, and even that was difficult."

"She was, unfortunately, an imprudent woman," Vera Vladimirovna answered, "and didn't know how to keep the love of her husband to whom she was indebted for her whole fortune."

"Not a very large fortune," Dmitry Ivachinsky remarked, "six hundred souls."

"Including ones from Kostroma," added a fat gentleman who owned peasants from Tambov and Yaroslav.

"It's lucky that there are no children," another lady said. "Stentsov will probably marry again."

"Yes, and we have already guessed to whom," said the fat gentleman, with an unbearably meaningful laugh.

During this conversation, Cecily had been seated by the window at her lace-frame. Dmitry Ivachinsky got up from where he was sitting and drew near that window, to Nadezhda Ivanovna who was sitting nearby, and began to say something to her, all the while looking fixedly and persistently at the empty stool near Cecily.

No mother can explain rhetoric of this kind, but every daughter can understand it. Cecily slowly raised her eyes with a favorable, silent answer to the humble question, and then suddenly dropped them in a severe and guarded way. Opposite her, leaning against the door to the balcony, stood Prince Victor, with a barely perceptible smile and a disturbing glance. The obedient Dmitry remained behind Nadezhda Ivanovna's chair, and the prince slowly assumed a dignified manner, walked directly to the sacred stool, and sat down on it without asking permission to do so. Cecily bent her blushing face to some flowers standing near her and, taking a long time to choose, picked a sprig of heliotrope. The prince began to speak of the previous day's vaudeville and the forthcoming horse race. Cecily could not possibly do anything but listen and answer. The prince, while speaking, carelessly stretched out his hand to the lace-frame, where Cecily was toying with the torn-off sprig, and took it. Vera Vladimirovna, sitting quietly in her long armchair, was unobserved following all his movements. The ladies present saw just as artfully as she everything to which they were paying no attention, but all were sufficiently wise and knew that it befits a prudent mother to act with severity only with impoverished suitors, and that the laws of the most refined conventionality are out of place with one who can give in exchange for a flower he has taken a half million in yearly income.

After ten minutes or so, the prince yawned slightly, got up, bowed imperceptibly, went out, and sped away in his foreign carriage, in his foreign clothes, with his foreign wit, leaving the crumpled sprig of heliotrope on the floor and the humiliated Dmitry next to Nadezhda Ivanovna.

Cecily, from her window, looked out after the spirited black horses carrying him away in a cloud of dust. Did she regret inwardly that Dmitry had no such equipage? Did she notice that his Russian coachman decidedly did not stand comparison with the prince's

English groom? Did she think that all other women would envy the one among them who could fly past them in that fascinating creation of London "high fashion . . ."? She glanced up for only a minute and bent over her sewing.

In the drawing room, a fairly lively argument was in progress:

"A most absurd wedding," someone said.

"She acted very cleverly," asserted one lady. "Their fortune was completely dissipated; the estate was supposed to be auctioned off. There was a mass of debts. She found herself a son-in-law who would restore and pay for everything."

"Monsieur Chardet!" answered one of the men in the group.

"Yes, it was Monsieur Chardet," she exclaimed. "He's really a very respectable man."

"But are you sure he is rich?"

"Of course. He has done some very profitable business. Sophia will be very happy with him."

"He gave her a marvelous emerald necklace," another lady said. "I saw it yesterday."

"It's still not a pleasant means of rescue."

"Pardon me, but you are behind the times. What do aristocratic prejudices mean in such a case! *Mésalliances* are very much in fashion now. George Sand has lent a kind of charm to ordinary people."

"Are you really a follower of George Sand?" Dmitry Ivachinsky asked her with a smile.

"To a certain extent: I like the folk element a good deal."

"With the exception of their raw sheepskin coats," he remarked.

"Well, yes, of course. But in fact there are marvelous peasants; one can meet them with pleasure, only naturally not as guests in one's own house."

Meanwhile time passed. Vera Vladimirovna's drawing room grew empty.

"Cécile," she said, "I have to go to the funeral now. You stay here with Miss Stevenson. I may be returning late. I'll probably be spending the evening with Natalia Afanasevna at Madame Stentsova's mother's house and somewhere else as well. So don't wait up for me, and go to bed at a decent hour. You are still not well. Goodbye, dear!"

Vera Vladimirovna went off with Nadezhda Ivanovna, and Cecily remained alone with Miss Stevenson—in other words, completely alone. She was decidedly not herself. What was weighing on her spirit she could not explain, nor did she try very hard. She didn't put to herself the only essential question: she didn't ask herself whether in fact she loved Dmitry Ivachinsky. According to her understanding, there was no room for doubt about this. But she didn't know what she had to do, how to attain the fulfillment of her wishes, how to go about it. If she had been capable of understanding that true feeling cannot hesitate and waver, that from the moment that consciousness becomes real and clear, action is equally clear and real because it has become a necessity and necessity knows no impediments; if she had been taught to look a truth in the face, if she could have guessed what it means to love. . . . But how was this possible when not only feeling itself, not only an understanding of what it was, but the very word had always been kept remote from her and cast aside like a tainted thing? Everything strove to suppress all spiritual strength in her, to kill all inner life. But still her young breast was not able to unlearn to tremble, and her heart could not renounce life and love, and her exacting, impatient soul was ready to embrace a cloud and a phantom instead of a heavenly being. At present, she vaguely and unconsciously sensed something false, but what and where? Whether in her inner or outer life, this was something she did not dare to seek out and explain. . . . Alas, her whole life was just one long and uninterrupted lie!

Toward evening, her slightly feverish condition grew worse. Miss Stevenson advised her to drink a raspberry cordial and lie down. She lay down. Incoherent thoughts wandered through her head. She remembered the ride to Ostankino and that morning and Prince Victor and that poor woman who had just been buried, who just a few days ago had been sitting before her, intense and happy. . . . It was getting late . . . she became lost in thought. For a long time, she looked into the half-darkness of the bedroom; but the evening grew dark, the room began to disappear before her eyes, and finally it did disappear, and a broad darkness fell . . . but something far off glimmered and grew light . . . and many faces and many lights were there . . . and meanwhile in the shadows, mysteriously hidden, *his* barely distinct breath wafted over her once more. . . .

And meanwhile a discordant noise was heard again,
The crowd pressed close within the dazzling rooms,
Wine flowed—the funeral feast progressed,
And the hum around the tables spread and grew.
And loud words took the place of toneless speech,
Smiles came to life, slander woke from sleep,
Worldly vanity, irresistible,
Knocked boldly even on the coffin's wood.

And there, in the distance, the moon came up;
And there, in the obscurity of night
The new grave shone black,
Already forgotten by the crowd.

And lime trees, whispering among themselves
In a language no one understands,
Softly swayed their heads
In their secret anguish.
And the meadow was drenched
In heavy tears of dew,
And in the twilight mist
Two furrows gleamed white.
Near the grave, two puffs of air
Drifted in the empty darkness;
Two voices merged, despondent,
With the murmuring leaves on the hill.

First Voice:

And you have crossed your arms in the coffin,
Leaving behind the noise of the world,
And all the struggles, all the partings,
All the strivings of the Earth!
You too, poor thing, were searching for
A pure pearl in the sea of life
And you died in vain, sorrowfully,
Victim of a ruinous dream!

Second Voice:

And did she enter into this world
To live an empty life and die a useless death?
And is the blind loss of will not sinful,

And is the power of crazed thought not shameful?
Where is her tribute? Where her cause in life?
How can her soul be reconciled with the Earth?
Did she look boldly into the face of fate?
Didn't she lie even to herself?
Didn't she lose heart at the power of an inner summons?
Did she fulfill the task entrusted to her?
Did she go forth? Did she seek the word of life?
Was she stronger than her sorrow?

First Voice:

The yoke of Earth's constraints
She did not bear on Earth,
Did not fall prey to doubt,
Did not take fright in the battle.
She loved sorrowfully and passionately,
Believing in the love of others,
And waited to the end in vain,
And hoped until the end.

Second Voice:

Why murmur against eternal laws?
Why not recognize the limits of the possible?
Groans are no substitute for holy labor,
Life is better than dreams and truth higher than lies.
Who is to blame that she had not the strength
To face the path, measure its steepness,

Not expect miracles, understand people from the first
And count only on herself!
Why, meeting deception every day,
Did she not renounce false faith
And why in the ruinous alchemy of the soul
Did she squander its store of wealth?

First Voice:

Stronger than insult, stronger than deception
Was the sacred fire of love in her.
Her wound could not subside,
Her sad gift could not disappear.
Who knew in that falsely rigorous world
Where grief is shameful and a joke,
How inconsolably she wept,
Resigned, before God,
What sacrifices she made,
What questions filled her heart,
In what storm her sail was sundered
After holding out so long?
No! If one has searched obscurely
For something which in life cannot be found,
If after hundreds of deceptions
One still could keep a blessed hope intact,
And measure with his soul on Earth
A surfeit of those superearthly powers,
One is not to blame for believing,
One is not to blame for loving.

06

The day was drawing near that Vera Vladimirovna always celebrated—Cecily's birthday. This time, too, she had made various preparations to spend the day as gaily as possible: a dinner, a concert, a *bal champêtre*, a supper—every possible thing that could be done was done, with great effort and at great expense. The festivity of people of the highest circles is wondrously expensive. When Cecily woke up that day, she found her mother's gifts lying on her sofa: two charming dresses—one a dinner dress, the other an evening dress—and the most marvelous lace scarf, ordered from Paris. In the course of the morning, she received approximately two dozen bouquets and three dozen notes from friends—all saying precisely the same thing, to which it was necessary to respond with precisely the same variations. Society women have achieved the wondrous art of contriving thirty variations on a phrase that means nothing even the first time. Then Madame Valitskaia arrived with her daughter (on that morning, no other people were received). Cecily went into the garden with Olga to rest from her correspondence a bit. They settled into a far corner, where there was a bit of shade, and began to chatter away; they talked of twenty different subjects, and then Olga's voice grew lower and more mysterious.

"Listen," she said, "you're killing Ivachinsky. He was so upset by your coolness yesterday that out of desperation, he lost all night at cards at Ilichev's and almost went out of his mind."

"Who told you that?" Cecily asked.

"My cousin told it to Mama. He was there and saw Dmitry. You're really driving him to goodness knows what. He's becoming a gambler."

It was not Olga herself who was saying these things—it was her mother's prompting. Only Madame Valitskaia knew the great power and naivete of female vanity; only Madame Valitskaia knew how much more interesting to a woman a man becomes, and how much dearer, the moment she sees the possibility of changing him after her own fashion, reforming him from vice, saving him from destruction. The greater the danger, the deeper the abyss ready to swallow him; the more glorious the triumph, the more tempting the success, and the greater the pleasure in stretching out to the one who is perishing a saving hand, fragile and yet all-powerful. Madame Valitskaia had decided that Cecily must become Dmitry's wife so that she would not somehow become the wife of Prince Victor, and she was proceeding toward her goal. Olga, for her part, was also of a mind to keep the precious prince for herself and did not trust Cecily much in this respect. Although Olga was too young to think up what levers to pull, she was clever enough to use them according to her mother's directions. In society's lexicon, this sort of move is called *adroit* or *clever*.

Instead of answering, Cecily bowed her head and fell to thinking. But that day, she had no time for lengthy reflection; the time to dress for dinner was approaching. Madame Valitskaia and her daughter left so that they too could dress and return in a couple of hours, and Cecily went to her room, called the maid, and sat down at her dressing table, loosening her black braids. She was so full of thoughts and daydreams that she paid no attention to her hair, over which the maid Annushka was laboring. Looking into her mirror, she thought only of what Olga had said. So she was capable of bringing Dmitry to desperation!—a possibility always flattering and satisfying to a woman, as a result of which she began to await him with great impatience.

But however much these thoughts possessed her, she could not help but be distracted, if only briefly, while putting on the splendid new dress. And indeed, when she was all ready and standing before her mirror, the reflection presented such a picture of grace that, looking at it, she understood perfectly poor Dmitry's torments of the heart.

The dinner was, like all dinners of this sort, long and boring. Aside from Vera Vladimirovna's husband and two or three guests like him, who ate with great appetite, everyone was waiting for it to end—Cecily and Olga more than anyone because Prince Victor and Dmitry were not expected until evening. Once dinner was over, they could still have a couple of pleasant hours to themselves.

The time for the concert finally arrived. The guests, whose number had increased, pressed into the room and began listening very patiently to variations and fantasias, arias and duets, accompanied by the constant movement of chairs set down for new arrivals. An Italian duet sung by Olga and Cecily ended the concert. It was delightful, of course, since it had been taken from the latest opera, and of course it gave the listeners enormous pleasure. A ripple passed through all three rows of toques and mob-caps in front of the pianos. All the men, mercilessly squeezed into the corners and

along the walls, clapped their hands in a storm of delight. Dmitry
Ivachinsky, who had just come in, was so unsparing of himself that
he tore his gloves to shreds. Prince Victor himself applauded more
than when he had heard Grisi in Paris. The duet, in short, produced
a huge effect, after which everyone dispersed into the garden with
sincere delight.

Cecily took Olga by the arm and ran with her toward her own
room in order to escape the general gratitude, correct her hair, and
change for the ball. In the doorway stood Dmitry Ivachinsky. He
bowed to her and whispered five or six words. Cecily nodded her
head and passed swiftly by.

"Olga," she said, after running upstairs to her room and smooth-
ing the dark waves of her hair before the mirror, "are you engaged for
the mazurka?"

"Since yesterday morning," Olga answered in a voice so content that
one could have no doubt as to whom she was promised. "And you?"

"Since just a minute ago," Cecily said, even more content, throw-
ing her marvelous scarf on the sofa.

She felt extraordinarily happy, somehow wildly and boldly happy.
She gave herself over to new, enthralling impressions. She was dimly
aware of certain unknown possibilities. The daughter of Eve was
tasting the forbidden fruit. The young captive was breathing in free,
fragrant, unfamiliar air, and it intoxicated her. This was something
that Vera Vladimirovna had never wished to foresee. Those prudent,
vigilant, cautious women never do. They rely totally on their mater-
nal efforts. They are extremely consistent with their daughters. In
place of the spirit, they give them the letter; in place of living, feeling
a dead rule; in place of holy truth, a preposterous lie. And they often
manage through these clever, precautionary machinations to steer

their daughters safely to what is called "a good match." Then their goal is attained. Then they leave her, confused, powerless, ignorant, and uncomprehending, to God's will; and afterward they sit down tranquilly to dinner and lie down to sleep. And this is the very same daughter whom at the age of six, they could not bring themselves to leave alone in a room, lest she fall off a chair. But that was a matter of bodily injuries—bloodshot eyes, frightening, physical pain—not of an obscure, mute pain of the spirit.

One could be consoled if only bad mothers acted in this way: there are not many bad mothers. But it is the very best mothers who do it and will go on doing it forever. And all these educators had been young once, and had been brought up in the same way! Were they really so satisfied with their own lives and with themselves that they are happy to renew the experience with their children? Is all this absurdity as long-lived as those reptiles that continue to exist after they are cut into pieces? Didn't these poor women weep? Didn't they blame themselves and other people? Didn't they look for help in vain? Didn't they feel the meaninglessness of the support given them? Didn't they recognize the bitter fruit of this lie?

But many of them, perhaps, did not! There are incredible cases and strange exceptions. There are examples of people falling from the third floor onto the pavement and remaining unharmed; then why not give one's daughter, too, a shove?

And it also must be said that so much is forgotten in life, the years change and reshape us so strangely! So many young, inspired dreamers in time become tax-farmers and distillers. So many carefree young idlers become owners of Siberian gold mines. So many frivolous scoundrels become merciless punishers of any enthusiasm. Time is a strange force!

When the friends came downstairs together in their ball gowns and appeared among the guests, they were truly beautiful. Olga, in a white dress of exceedingly expensive simplicity, with cornflowers in her long, blond curls, was astonishingly lovely; but Cecily, who was also all in white, with a crown of white roses set over her proud black braids, was even lovelier. Olga was still searching for something; Cecily had already found it. Olga glowed with hope; Cecily shone with victory. In her face, her smile, her whole glance, her every movement, there was something even too beautiful for good form, something splendidly ravishing, a kind of victory at Poltava. And this was only the shadow of love! But love is so inexpressibly ravishing that even its shadow is full of charm and better than anything else.

The weather was most propitious. The starry night breathed a marvelous, life-giving warmth. The ball, or rustic ball, as it was called, was modeled on a celebration recently given in Paris and quite in the new fashion. The carefully rolled courtyard in front of the entrance to the house served as a ballroom. It was tightly encircled by a double row of laurels and orange trees and tall, rare flowers. Among the branches, gas lamps were burning, pouring their bright light onto the whole scene. The adjacent garden was also illuminated, but more dimly, with small flames in translucent porcelain globes and alabaster vases. It had been transformed into a drawing room, withdrawing rooms, and a buffet. Opulent furniture was artfully arranged throughout. Tea tables were standing under fragrant shrubs. Pyramids of fruit rose in the middle of multicolored dahlias and beautiful camellias composed into luxuriant bunches. Mysterious lights glowed fantastically through the dark green. All this was indeed amazingly fine.

From behind a thick mass of acacias, an invisible orchestra struck up and the ball began. Thanks to that unusual setting and the attractive novelty of it all, the decorous, indolent, aristocratic company came unexpectedly to life. Dances followed swiftly one after the other. At times, light, feminine laughter was heard in the night air. Everything was movement, noise, and gaiety. The tranquil stars looked down from their heights; a few old trees stood in sullen silence, gloomy and motionless among the crowd.

Time passed. The dances continued. Cecily, who always tired quickly, felt no fatigue that evening. A new, inexplicable existence was growing in her. One of those rich hours of life had struck when the heart is so self-confident that no happiness is capable of taking it by surprise. At that moment, a miracle would have seemed natural and ordinary to her: she would not even have paid it any attention. If one of those shining stars had fallen to Earth before her, she would have simply pushed it away with her foot.

Providence sometimes bestows such moments on earthly existence!

It was close to midnight. The party, as always happened around this time, reached its most brilliant moment. There was noise and movement everywhere. Everywhere through the greenery glimmered dresses of different colors, floating scarves, and glittering bracelets on white arms. Everywhere voices were heard: jokes, mockery, compliments, slander, the vulgarity of some, the wit of others, the coquetry of still others—all mixed and blended into one general sound. From its fathomless darkness, the night sky shone strangely above this turmoil. Those drawing-room speeches, those empty words sounded somehow insolent in the dark infinity; the worldly, false, "civilized" life sounded somehow sinful and sacrilegious in God's free expanse.

After many quadrilles, Olga, Cecily, and another young girl sat down to rest, the three of them on a small divan in a cozy, half-hidden corner of the garden. Dmitry Ivachinsky came up to them and began to talk with the third girl; she laughed and answered him animatedly. Suddenly, the mazurka started. Olga took her neighbor who had been talking with Dmitry by the hand and ran off with her. Cecily also stood up, took a couple of steps, looked around, and stopped. For a minute, she was alone with Ivachinsky.

"Dmitry Andreevich," she said suddenly, with a charming blush, "I have a request to make of you: don't play cards as you did yesterday at Ilichev's. You will promise, won't you? You won't gamble any more?"

"I won't," he answered, "if you'll give me that flower you tore off your bouquet and are holding in your hand."

The mazurka thundered louder. Cecily flitted through the garden, but the flower fell from her hand onto the path.

She stopped for a second, at the turning of the path: did she really have to look to see if he would find it? The flower was in the hand of Dmitry, who was following her. She stretched out her own hand a little, with the sincere intention of taking it back, but her look was more honest than her hand. There was no one in the garden. Dmitry grasped her outstretched fingers and swiftly kissed them.

Two minutes later, she began dancing the mazurka with him and slipped into the bright circle, surrounded by chairs, among the crowd of onlookers. But who among them could see how tenderly that trembling little hand, which had been kissed for the first time, was grasped?

It was the same simple story once again, old and forever new! It was true that Dmitry was captivated by Cecily. The magnetism of other people's opinions always had an astonishing effect on him.

Seeing her that evening, so dazzling and so surrounded, he could not fail to be satisfied with her and far more satisfied with himself. He was one of those weak creatures who grow drunk on success. At that moment, he was no longer merely calculating: he saw himself placed higher than all the rest by Cecily, higher even than Prince Victor, the arrogant object of his secret envy; and his head began to turn. Inside him started up youth's wildness and its irresistible burst of passion, as at the height of battle, when the warrior rushes blindly forward to tear the standard from the enemy ranks at any cost. It really did resemble love, perhaps mixed with some attraction of the heart as well, but this was only that ruthless masculine feeling which, if the woman inspiring him had committed some awkwardness, had worn some unattractive coiffure or unfashionable hat, could at any moment change into fierce malice.

But one could lay odds that Cecily was incapable of committing the slightest awkwardness and would always be perfectly dressed and coiffed.

The mazurka ended at last. Supper was waiting on various tables, large and small, placed about the garden. Cecily and Dmitry sat as far as they could from one another. They now intentionally kept their distance; they were already two conspirators hiding their association.

The party was coming to a close. Coaches and carriages were brought round. As Madame Valitskaia had requested, Dmitry found her carriage and escorted her to it. While they were walking, he bent toward her a little and whispered in a voice full of meaning:

"Permit me to call on you tomorrow morning, Natalia Afanasevna. For I have to request of you an important service."

"I will expect you with great pleasure," she answered. "Come after midday."

The lackey opened the doors of the carriage. Madame Valitskaia sat down feeling almost as lively and happy as her daughter.

The short summer night was already turning pale by the time the guests had all left. It may be said that everyone (or nearly everyone at least) was satisfied. They had rushed about, danced, made noise, and amused themselves to the point of exhaustion. For her part, Vera Vladimirovna lay down to sleep quite satisfied. Her party had been a complete success, and Prince Victor had looked at Cecily often and had twice declared that she was extremely lovely. Madame Valitskaia also lay down to sleep very satisfied: just one more little push was needed to get that dangerous Cecily out of the way. Olga went to bed even more satisfied: the prince had talked a lot of nonsense to her during the mazurka and had remarked that her dress was exceptionally becoming. Dmitry could not be dissatisfied: his vanity was still running high and, as he fell asleep, he felt inwardly victorious. Prince Victor always went to bed completely satisfied with himself and with others. Finally, even poor Nadezhda Ivanovna—who never succeeded in anything, who never arranged anything or expected anything, whom no one danced with or spoke to—even she fell asleep extremely satisfied, for no reason at all.

But Cecily lay down to sleep with the abounding happiness that sometimes fills an eighteen-year-old heart for a moment, and that is so alive that in quiet and solitude, it becomes almost painful. She could not think, but there was turmoil in her breast, and dreams flickered. Her closed eyes still saw the ball, the bright-colored crowd, and the illuminated garden. And her drowsing consciousness grew inexplicably somber with some unaccountable feeling. Happy, she sighed mournfully, not knowing why. And a languorous drowsiness descended comfortingly on her. It was as if echoes of the orchestra were still drifting through the silence—distant, half-sorrowful harmonies, now stopping, now starting up again, and melting into strange talk, mysterious conversations, marvelous, wished-for sounds, *his* call, into *his* greeting:

"The far-off star
Has long been flaming;
Long have I waited,
The hour goes by.
Languishing in an evil dream
In that strange land,
Awake, beloved,
In your own country;
Among the victorious
Sacred things of night,
Leave the deception
Of material worry."

Sad is the smile on his lips,
His words flow more gently:

"O, eternal error of the heart,
How early you have grown close to her!
How soon the voice of bold convictions
Has been awakened in her!
How many painful revelations,
How many sorrows lie ahead!
How life will try in vain to disenchant
Her soul to the very end!

Alas! There in the world all is unclear,
There all is blind and false raving!
With dark, mute thought, you
Will search for me alone:
It is in me your soul believes,
Me that you love, not him.
But in the midst of changing vanity
In your routine of every day,
I will remain an unclear sadness,
A dream of the heart unrealized.
And sensing light in the depths of gloom,
Trusting in an unearthly secret,
You will travel from ghost to ghost,
From one sorrow to another.
In everything that will be dear to your heart,
In everything you will see the same lie;
You have not loved the infinite,
You wait for the immeasurable.
It is not life, O fateful thirsting,
That will assuage your pain!
You will have a different future,
Different streams of life.
So let stern fate take its course,
The bright paradise of hopes vanishes!
Get used to a difficult path
And learn the strength of the weak.
Understand that the Lord's Commandments
Have doomed you, defenseless ones,
To unconditional patience

To a task higher than that on Earth.

Learn, as a woman, the suffering of a woman,

Know that, submissive, she

Must not seek the path

To her own dreams, her own desires;

That her heart protests in vain,

That her duty is implacable,

That all her soul is in his power,

That even her thoughts are fettered by him.

Prepare all the strength of youth

For mute tears, for an obscure struggle,

And may the heavenly father give you

An unconquerable love!"

07

T he following morning, even before midday, Natalia Afanasevna was sitting on her terrace. On the little table in front of her stood a cup of chocolate and the latest of Alexandre Dumas's countless novels; but the cup with its delicious beverage remained full and the book by the absorbing storyteller unopened. Madame Valitskaia was in no mood for chocolate or stories just now: she was preparing the denouement to the prologue of a certain real-life novel of great interest to her. She leaned her elbows meditatively on her soft armchair, took a watch from under the sash of her peignoir and cast a momentary glance at it, then from time to time got up, walked to one side of the terrace from where she could see the broad avenue of the park, and looked through her lorgnette into the dusty distance. Returning dissatisfied to her armchair for the third or fourth time, she began toying impatiently with the little knife with a mother-of-pearl handle that was placed in the book.

Steps were heard, and Nadezhda Ivanovna appeared on the terrace, very red and exhausted.

"Where have you been?" asked Natalia Afanasevna.

"Walking with Olga almost halfway around the park. We're all tired out."

"Why do you go walking in the heat? Where is Olga?"

"She went with Miss Jeffries to her room. As we were coming back, we met some young people—Sofia Chardet and her husband. They were in a carriage."

"Indeed?"

"Yes, she was wearing a marvelous cloak."

"Have you sent to find out about Katerina Vasilevna's health?"

"Yes; they still haven't returned with an answer."

Again Madame Valitskaia glanced at her watch. While continuing to ask empty questions out loud, inwardly she was asking herself completely different, uneasy ones: "Surely he hasn't had second thoughts and won't be coming? Impossible. How shall I manage Vera Vladimirovna? She won't agree: it's not a fantastic match. Will I really not be able to handle this? I have to think up something! But what?"

A swift droshky pulled up with a clatter and stopped. It was Dmitry.

At that exact moment, as if it were called forth by the clatter of the wheels, Madame Valitskaia was struck with a sudden, completely unexpected, bold, and magnificent idea.

"Nadezhda Ivanovna," she said hurriedly, "please tell them to harness up the carriage for me, and leave me alone with Ivachinsky. I have to talk over some business with him. Tell them not to receive any visitors. And not to come in to announce when the carriage is ready; I will ring for it myself. Go on now."

The obedient Nadezhda Ivanovna, fulfilling her almost daily duty, went out, and Dmitry Ivachinsky came in.

Madame Valitskaia extended her hand to him in a friendly manner.

"Natalia Afanasevna," he said, "I have come to you with a most important request."

"I'm ready to do everything possible," she interrupted approvingly.

"It's a question of my life's happiness," he continued. "I am speaking to you directly and without preparation: I love Cecily Alexandrovna. I fell in love with her long ago; I have been hiding it for more than a year. But I can hide it no longer."

Dmitry was always carried away by his own words. One could say that he did not control them, but rather the opposite. From this fact, there sometimes resulted something resembling lies.

"I guessed your secret long ago," Natalia Afanasevna answered in her kindly voice.

"I beg you," he added, "help me to reach this happiness! Take it upon yourself to convey my request to Vera Vladimirovna. Try to win her over. Be my Providence."

"Are you sure that Cecily loves you?" she asked.

"I have reason to presume so," he answered with a smile that gave a measure of his mind.

"I thought so myself; but you see, Dmitry Andreevich, this whole business is very difficult. Let's speak openly with one another. There's an impediment here: Prince Victor. . . ."

"Prince Victor!" Dmitry burst out with proud scorn, not having the strength to refrain from the pleasure of pronouncing this name in such a tone for the first time.

"Yes, Prince Victor, although I am completely convinced that he has never thought seriously about Cecily as a bride for himself. . . ."

"He may have thought about her," Dmitry interrupted again with an arrogant quip, "but she has certainly not thought about him."

Madame Valitskaia assumed her well-known expression that might mean anything at all, and continued:

"Perhaps, but he flirts with her all the same, and her mother hopes that a wedding will follow from this. His huge fortune tempts her against her will. I, for my part, have never thought of seeking wealth in choosing a husband for Olga, but Vera Vladimirovna is of another mind on that score. I don't know if I can be of use to you in this business."

"Natalia Afanasevna! Have mercy! Don't refuse me your aid. You alone can arrange it all. You are so close to Vera Vladimirovna. Convince her to agree to our happiness! This love is mutual. Cecily will be unhappy with another husband, as I will be with another wife. Vera Vladimirovna truly does not wish her daughter to be miserable, nor would you. Surely you'd be delighted to accept in a case like this if it were Olga Alexeevna?"

"Fool!" Natalia Afanasevna thought.

"I cannot judge others as I would myself," she said sweetly, "and have no right to demand that they share my feelings and opinions. I have different conceptions of life's happiness, and in such circumstances, I would naturally not hesitate for a moment if I were in Vera Vladimirovna's place. But I am afraid that she is not like me in this respect. On the other hand, I sincerely wish you success. But in order to attain it, you must go about things extremely cautiously. You see, I am of course very friendly with Vera Vladimirovna, but I have almost no influence over her. In order to put forth your proposition to her, we have to find someone whose opinion might influence her, someone who might command her respect. Let me think . . . well, yes, who better? . . . Only, will she do it?"

"Who might that be?" Dmitry asked.

"None other than Princess Anna Sergeevna, Prince Victor's mother. Her request will carry a good deal of weight, and success would almost be guaranteed. Only it will be difficult to persuade her; you do not know her very well."

"But you know her very well, Natalia Afanasevna. Can't you ask her?"

"Yes, perhaps she won't say no to me. By the way, she loves to arrange weddings. Let us try! I want to justify fully your faith in me. Would you like me to take you to her right now so that I may try to persuade her?"

"Natalia Afanasevna, I'm unutterably grateful to you. How kind you are!"

"I'm always sincerely happy to do a service for my friends," she said, "especially such an important service. It's a question of your happiness; I will do my utmost."

She rang; a manservant entered.

"My carriage in ten minutes," ordered Natalia Afanasevna. "Wait for me here," she continued, turning to Ivachinsky, "I'll be ready in a minute."

Indeed, she returned in a very short time, dressed and wearing a hat, and the carriage was brought so quickly that one might have guessed that it had been standing there, already harnessed. Madame Valitskaia and Dmitry got into it and set off to see Princess Anna Sergeevna.

On the way, Natalia Afanasevna, leaning back in the corner of the carriage, kept silent or responded absentmindedly to what Ivachinsky was saying. The idea on whose outcome she was already acting was still lying obscure and undeveloped within her. This had been a sudden insight, one of those strokes of genius that never deceive us, however unreal and strange they may appear: you believe in success, not yet seeing its possibility and not yet understanding its realization. Now she was thinking everything through, clarifying all the details, and preparing the whole scene in her head, and she understood more and more that the affair would run smoothly, that the unbelievable would happen, that chance would not alter it, that no circumstance, no grain of sand would hinder its success. This success was hanging by a thread and could be destroyed by a single word; but Madame Valitskaia had a presentiment that the thread would not break, that the word would not be spoken. This was the sixth sense of the intriguer, similar to the clairvoyance of the great.

They arrived, they were announced, they were received. The old princess was very busy with the inspection and selection of new material for dresses. But for Madame Valitskaia's sake, she cut short her profound deliberations with the French mademoiselle who was spreading out enticing goods before her, and, sending her away, she ordered her to return with them that evening so that she could judge the effect of the materials by candlelight. Then she turned to greet Natalia Afanasevna.

"Princess!" the latter began. "Knowing how kind you are, I took the liberty of bringing you a young man to whose happiness you can contribute. I was convinced in advance that you would not refuse."

"Delighted," muttered the princess, not yet understanding and not recognizing Ivachinsky.

"Dmitry Andreevich Ivachinsky," said Madame Valitskaia, introducing him. "You have met him socially."

"Delighted," the princess repeated haughtily.

"Permit me to go into your boudoir with you," Natalia Afanas-evna continued. "It will take no more than five minutes for me to explain the reason for our visit. I know that you are always glad of the opportunity to do a good deed. In the meantime, you wait here, Dmitry Andreevich."

She went into her boudoir with the princess, who, to tell the truth, was not at all so predisposed to good deeds and favors as Madame Valitskaia had asserted. But it is very hard to contradict such assertions and convictions, and for the princess, it was even harder.

Princess Anna Sergeevna had somehow divined—God knows through what revelation—that in order to be a complete woman, one should add to wealth some other ingredient. Meanwhile, profoundly despising intellectual abilities and talents (which always seemed to her to be signs of something plebeian), having long since lost her former claim to eminence—beauty—and, what is more, understanding that at her age, it was no longer a great virtue to be virtuous, she had decided as old age approached to be kind. This came at an unbelievably great cost to her egotistical nature, but she persisted and had finally acquired the reputation of someone who was impossibly kind. Taking advantage of this, Madame Valitskaia found it very easy to convince her, although at first, the princess did not quite understand why she had to take such an interest in this Ivachinsky and go off and make a match for him. But Natalia Afanasevna was a past mistress in such cases: once she was alone with the princess, she explained the whole matter to her perfectly and made her understand.

"You see, Princess, these poor children love one another passionately, but Vera Vladimirovna is looking for a brilliant match for her daughter, and the young man is not wealthy."

"Not everyone can be wealthy," the princess very justly remarked.

"That is absolutely true! Nevertheless, Vera Vladimirovna does not wish Cecily to marry him. But she esteems and respects you so much that . . ."

The princess's face was saying: I should certainly hope she respects me!

"Your opinion," the advocate continued, "carries such weight that she is bound to agree if only you could undertake to talk to her about this matter. You understand that she would find it awkward to refuse you."

"Of course," the princess agreed.

"And so, you will ride over and sacrifice an hour in order to arrange the happiness of two hearts and save them from despair. I didn't doubt for a minute your readiness to fulfill my request."

"Very well," the princess answered, "I might as well go immediately: one should not postpone a good deed."

"I guessed right about you," Natalia Afanasevna said. "But one more thing: you understand better than anyone how to make use of people's weaknesses in such instances." (Madame Valitskaia, saying this, was truly inimitable.) "You know how proud Vera Vladimirovna is of her maternal powers of perception, and she really does follow all the feelings and actions of her daughter uncommonly closely. She would be extremely offended if you were to speak to her of this mutual love as of an event unknown to her, and if you even considered it necessary to mention the young man's name. Naturally, you will only hint to her about him so as not to insult the main core of her self-esteem. She will understand you as soon as you start speaking and will be very content to show you that she has understood and that nothing concerning Cecily can be hidden from her. What can you do? She is such a kind woman that one can forgive her this small bit of maternal vanity."

"Naturally," said the princess, "and I will try to spare her."

"You are always so tactful," Madame Valitskaia continued, "and know so well how to act with everyone! You know that in order to win over Vera Vladimirovna, one should not give her advice; she doesn't like it."

"I know," answered the princess. "I will simply tell her that I have taken it upon myself to seek her consent."

"Exactly," said Natalia Afanasevna.

They came out together into the drawing room, where the impatient Dmitry was waiting. The princess accepted the eloquent outpourings of his gratitude and ordered her carriage.

"Don't worry," she repeated, seating herself in it, "I will arrange everything and will send you word."

"I am sure, princess," Natalia Afanasevna replied, "that you will act with extraordinary skill and will forget nothing that might lead to our goal. You have knowledge of the heart."

With this, the princess set forth, already very satisfied with her own magnanimous selflessness, which had enticed her to ride out in such heat, across almost the whole park, for another's benefit. And Natalia Afanasevna and Dmitry once more got into her carriage, and she could not help pronouncing somewhat inspiredly:

"Home!"

Vera Vladimirovna was ready to set forth on her usual visiting obligations when Princess Anna Sergeevna's arrival was announced to her. This was an unusual event: The princess rarely went out in the morning, and, having spent the whole previous evening at Vera Vladimirovna's, she surprised her very much by appearing again on the following day. Here was something to wonder about. Vera Vladimirovna hastened to meet her and invited her to sit down.

"I have not come to you today on a simple visit," the princess began. "I have taken upon myself a rather delicate business: I have been entrusted with making a proposal to you. . . ."

She stopped in order to take a pinch of snuff. Vera Vladimirovna shuddered inwardly as if from a galvanic shock. She dared not yet rejoice.

"The proposal concerns Cecily," the princess continued slowly. "You no doubt understand who I am talking about."

Vera Vladimirovna could not refrain from rejoicing.

"You probably noticed yesterday," the princess added and took another pinch of snuff.

"Indeed," Vera Vladimirovna said. "I did notice."

How could she not acknowledge this? She had in fact so vigilantly followed every word and step of Prince Victor in the course of the previous evening.

"Yes," the princess added, "I too saw something." (This would have demonstrated improbable powers of sight, because the princess had spent nearly the whole evening at the card table, in a special room.) "Of course," she continued, "you have already guessed about Cecily's love as well!"

If this had come from anyone else, Vera Vladimirovna would have been extremely offended by even the supposition that Cecily secretly loved someone. But the mother of Prince Victor herself was saying this. It was impossible for Vera Vladimirovna to contradict her. And besides, it was no longer a question of taking offense.

"A loving mother always guesses all the movements of her daughter's heart," she exclaimed with feeling, barely hiding her triumphant bliss.

"I think," said the princess, "that you have no objection."

Had these words been chosen by Madame Valitskaia herself, they could not have corresponded more closely with her aims. One could only regret that the bold instigator of this scene did not witness it.

"I never wanted to hamper Cecily," the tender mother answered. "She made her choice freely. Her upbringing was a guarantee to me that this choice would be approved by me."

"I assumed so," the princess said, "and I was convinced that you would not oppose this mutual love. And so, you agree?"

"Princess," Vera Vladimirovna answered, yielding to a very real temptation to make use of this auspicious moment, which allowed her to become with impunity a woman magnanimous and stoical, "I did not have wealth in mind for Cecily. I only wanted her to find a husband with spiritual virtues and a warm heart, a noble man in the true sense of the word. My wishes have been fulfilled; God has heard my prayer!"

"And so," the princess said, in conclusion, "I may go home with a satisfactory answer? You give your agreement?"

"I give it with sincere joy," Vera Vladimirovna assured her. "I could not wish for a better husband for my daughter. I know that she will be happy."

"Naturally," said the princess, "you are absolutely right. Money does not buy happiness."

"Could she want to deprive her son of his inheritance?" the frightened Vera Vladimirovna was thinking.

"Love conquers all," continued the princess, having once again taken recourse to her gold snuffbox. "Your Cecily will joyfully sacrifice empty superfluity and a few trivial habits. You have been so skilled in developing her ability to reason; even a moderate lot will satisfy her."

"What is this? What is this? . . ." the poor Vera Vladimirovna was thinking. "Lord, what does this mean? . . . Is she herself undertaking to remarry? The estate after all is hers alone. . . ."

She glanced at the princess. It was difficult to make such a supposition.

"And so," the princess said, getting up, "I will go home to reassure the young man, who impatiently awaits an answer. I am very happy for him. He pleaded so with me just now that I could not refuse undertaking to speak to you about his proposal, although at first this seemed to me not quite appropriate. Well, thank God! That's the end of it. And he, poor man, feared a refusal. But I knew that you would agree. You are such a good mother. And he, it seems, is a very respectable man. He has good acquaintances. He can enter any profitable career, find patronage, and make his way in life. I will tell Victor to help him. Well, then, goodbye."

Vera Vladimirovna was now completely in the dark. "So it isn't Prince Victor at all?" she asked herself with despair. "Well, who is it then?"

But it was impossible to make inquiries about the name of the man to whom she had agreed to give her daughter.

Embarrassed, she looked for a possibility of salvation and didn't find it; in her mind, all was confusion. Then it seemed that the means appeared to her for an instant, and she grasped at it with the eagerness of a dying person.

"Excuse me, princess," she said. "Haven't we been in too much of a hurry in this? I must have a serious talk with Cecily."

"Her love is known to you," the princess answered. "There is nothing to ask her."

"Of course . . . but even so . . . this is such an important step that a young girl must think it over thoroughly; it's so easy to make a mistake!"

"You were just saying that you could not wish for a better husband for Cecily."

"Of course . . . I am convinced . . . still . . . allow me to ask her. . . ."

The unhappy Vera Vladimirovna was becoming completely lost.

"If you please," said the princess, "speak with her, although this seems to me completely unnecessary. She will surely be ready to marry the man she loves. Goodbye."

Vera Vladimirovna was saved. She could settle accounts with Cecily; she could learn her secret, forbid her to think about this man of no means, annihilate this stupid love, and find some pretext, some excuse to refuse it. She was, of course, an exceedingly good mother, and she was always ready to fulfill the whims and desires of her daughter; but this was an altogether different matter—this was not a joke.

Swiftly grasping all this, somewhat reassured, she escorted the princess out.

Madame Valitskaia's brilliant plan had not succeeded. She had lost the affair in spite of her firm faith in success. In order that this faith might not deceive her, it was now necessary for some completely extraneous, unforeseen circumstance to present itself.

The circumstance appeared.

It could not have been otherwise! Napoleon was not killed by an infernal machine because a woman took it into her head to wear a different shawl.[1]

---

1. A reference to an assassination attempt on the rue Saint-Nicaise on December 24, 1800.

Madame Valitskaia also found her lucky star at that moment. The princess, accompanied by Vera Vladimirovna, was walking toward the door. This door opened, and Cecily entered in a cloak and hat, ready to ride with her mother.

"Well, here she is!" exclaimed the princess. "We shall ask her immediately. Listen, *ma chère enfant*, Ivachinsky is asking for your hand in marriage; your mother agrees; do you wish to marry him?"

Cecily blushed, grew pale again, and said in happy confusion, "If Mama agrees, I will be happy to!"

"There, you see," the princess joined in, "I was right. The poor children! Well, now everything is all right. I will send someone to tell him right away."

Vera Vladimirovna could not speak, could barely even understand.

The door opened again. Madame Valitskaia and Olga appeared as if called forth at this decisive moment. Her instinct had guided her as surely as the raven points its way to carrion.

No sooner had she entered than she was completely at ease: at one glance, she could guess everything.

"Congratulate Cecily," the princess told her. "She is Ivachinsky's fiancée."

Olga hugged her best friend; Madame Valitskaia clasped her good friend's hand with great feeling.

"You are a happy mother!" she told her.

Vera Vladimirovna began to cry.

The kind princess sent her carriage for Dmitry. He arrived. Everything followed the usual order. Everyone was very moved, especially Natalia Afanasevna. Even Vera Vladimirovna's husband came home. Madame Valitskaia, upon meeting him, immediately informed him of what had happened, and that the only thing lacking was his consent. He consented and gave his daughter his blessing.

Vera Vladimirovna shuddered with sudden vexation at herself: in her confusion, she had forgotten about her husband! He might have been a means of salvation if he had seemed not to want to give Cecily in marriage to Ivachinsky. Now it was already too late to grasp at this straw.

The princess was showered with blessings and praise. She let it be known that she was entirely content with her morning and named herself as sponsor at the wedding.

Dmitry Ivachinsky stayed to dine and entered into all the rights of a fiancé. Vera Vladimirovna was, like all women of good society, sufficiently educated and polished to assume when necessary an air that in no way corresponded to her inner feelings, and was able even now to observe all the proprieties in splendid fashion. For Cecily, this day went by in a state of joyous excitement; she could hardly believe in the truth of what had happened.

So she was really Dmitry's fiancée? The obstacles that had frightened her had vanished. The difficulties were all smoothed over. Her dream come true was within reach.

The evening went by extraordinarily rapidly. It was already late when Vera Vladimirovna sent Dmitry home.

Weary with happiness, Cecily entered her room. Mechanically, she began to undress, and mechanically, she got into bed with a single, ecstatic thought. A bountiful atmosphere of peaceful happiness surrounded her and gave her life. Every thought caressed, every feeling lulled her . . .

Her quiet smile met the dream that was growing nearer . . . It was already hovering over her . . .

And far away there were so many wonderful visions, bright joys . . .

And the wind barely whispers, softly wafting;
Through the mist of branches the moon looks on;
And the unending avenue of trees
Is full of the thick twilight.

Who, standing deep within,
Is seen briefly through the moonlit garden?
The mute shadow comes closer, blackly,
The starry glance shines brighter.

"Yes, I know, you are coming again;
Again you are looking into my heart;
Again your word will thunder forth,
And shatter my youthful dreams.

Sorrowful force, you always turn
My happiness to lies;
Like a flame burning in a censer,
You light a ray of thought in me.

Leave me alone, stern spirit!
You grow sadder and gloomier;
I fear your revelations,
Your pitiless love.

Let me accustom my soul
To its trivial daily lot:
I do not wish to foresee more,
No more do I wish to know!

Why do you tear in vain
Its mute prisoner from the world,
And teach an earthly being
To live without an earthly idol.

Should we really walk the path
Of Earth so anxiously and so in vain,
Love only what is impossible,
Only believe in what is far away?

Why could you not leave my heart
A brief day of deception?
Why give me this ruinous lesson
In advance, so early?"

"In order that you might discern
Where fateful eternity awaits;
That you might understand something other
Than that series of empty cares.

In order that the light of your soul
Might not go out in the dark of Earth;
In order that you not commit
Sacrilege upon yourself.

Arise out of the dust of life!
Calm the confusion in your heart!
Look without fear, immortal soul,
Into the face of truth!

Understand that all desires are vain,
That existence is a series of losses,
That its sacrifices have no recompense,
That its sufferings have no reward.

And feel that within you there is something
Inexplicable at present,
Higher than any calculation,
And any blessings, any losses!"

08

Following the memorable morning that so suddenly decided Cecily's fate, everything around her changed and came to life, as usually happens in the house of a bride-to-be. The days went by swiftly, one after the other, so filled up that they became completely empty. The ardent bridegroom, as is the custom, pleaded to hasten the wedding date; the prudent mother postponed it, asking for the time necessary for preparations. Vera Vladimirovna, seeing that there was now nothing to be done, proved that she was a very clever woman by deciding, to spite her foes and her friends, to be completely satisfied with this marriage, and using it as a frame into which she began to insert to great advantage a considerable portion of her virtues (unselfishness, magnanimity, maternal love, and so forth and so on), so she might have the pleasure of speaking fine phrases and receiving touching praise.

The house was taken over by merchants, shop assistants, upholsterers, Tatars, seamstresses, milliners. Samples, parcels, hatboxes, packages lay about everywhere. There was no end to congratulatory visits; excursions, dinners, evening parties succeeded one another. All that busy whirling pace of society life accelerated to the point where it made one's head spin. This state of lively tension, the jolly noise that surrounds brides, call to mind that accidentally deafening music and beating of drums by which soldiers are led into mortal combat. So little time remained to make the necessary arrangements. One had to worry about so many crucial details, peruse so many fashionable journals, choose from so many materials and fabrics of all kinds, talk so frequently with the diamond merchant and the goldsmith, try on so many dresses, peignoirs, cloaks, shawls, hats, mob-caps and headdresses—in short, be so occupied with the heart of the matter that not one free minute remained to muse idly upon any other thing.

And anyway, what was there to muse about, and to what purpose, especially for Cecily? Her wishes had been fulfilled, her secret dreams realized. Around her, all was bright and beautiful. She had reached those enchanting hours of life when the curtain on a marvelous future near at hand rises a little, minute by minute, allowing her chaste eyes to take a fleeting glimpse and her sensitive heart to tremble joyfully.

And it all was so new for her, so unexpected, so inconceivable. This whole world in which she suddenly found herself had always been kept so secret from her until now, so carefully put to one side and concealed, that her understanding could conceive of no comparison with anything similar, and she had to consider herself as some kind of blessed, magnificent exception to the general rule. Dmitry, moreover, did not modify the customary habits of fiancés, and as innocently and good-heartedly as all of them, led this ignorant, gullible soul from one deception to another, from delusion to delusion, each more consoling and delightful than the last. For the lies of a watchful mother he substituted the lies of a tender lover, saving the inexorable truth for the dicta of a stern husband. Wherever one looked, there was concession and flattery, merry faces and friendly words. Whatever was there to think over and contemplate? Precisely nothing. Everything was presented in a fine light; Cecily could not conceive of anything better.

Dmitry was not wealthy—in the understanding of society, he was almost poor—but even this very circumstance enhanced her pleasure. Despite everything she heard and saw, despite all the opinions expressed by everyone and all her mother's moral instruction, she (God knows why) unaccountably felt within herself that it was somehow nobler and better to prefer poverty to wealth, Ivachinsky to Prince Victor. She sincerely rejoiced in her choice. It is true that she understood poverty after her own fashion, as something refined, attractive, a kind of new outfit that would be very becoming to her; and already she was impatiently constructing in her mind a restricted way of life in which more money actually would be spent than in a luxurious one. She dreamed of how sweet it would be to live in poverty; to wear the simplest of dresses, sewn by Madame André, whose style would be worth twice as much as the material itself; to furnish small rooms with skill and elegance; to ride in a light, beautiful carriage, harnessed with only a pair of fine grays; even sometimes in good weather to walk with her husband in a smart cloak or in a velvet coat lined with ermine. Other constraints she did not know and could not imagine. Naturally, she sometimes noticed an ugly dress or the old, clumsy carriage of some other woman about whom it was said with insulting pity that she was poor; but this was indeed only ignorance, a lack of taste. How could it be possible not to be able to order a fashionable dress and own a decent carriage? What kind of poverty does not allow even that? It happened on her outings that she saw nasty hovels and met women in miserable, threadbare clothing, who in freezing weather were covered only with an old shawl, pale men in ragged overcoats, wasted children in repulsively filthy little shirts; but these were already inhabitants of another world—beings of another order with whom she could have nothing in common. She had before her eyes every day an example of another, perhaps even more pitiful existence, the striking example of drawing-room poverty—Nadezhda Ivanovna—but that was something totally different too, that was Nadezhda Ivanovna; but she didn't even come to mind.

And so what was there left for her to wish for? Dmitry was passionately in love with her, he was very good-looking, extraordinarily *comme il faut*, and perfectly educated and clever. He could not appear otherwise to her. She who had lived her whole life in this all-pervading atmosphere of banality could not be struck by Ivachinsky's banality, just as a pallid artisan who never leaves his dirty workshop does not notice the oppressive airlessness of his dwelling. Besides, even for a woman of broader outlook, it is not easy to identify the mediocre mind quickly amid the conventional, cultivated forms of society. How and by what means may one in an aristocratic drawing room distinguish the vulgar man from the brilliantly intelligent one? Surely only by the fact that the former usually seems more clever. Finally, in addition to everything else, Dmitry was unbelievably kind and impossibly meek, even almost too meek—the distinguishing trait of all future husbands, an excess that happily disappears later on.

So, again, what more could Cecily wish for? How could she not feel herself to be a blessed creature in the world? What did she lack?

Perhaps one thing: a few truths among all this fine phantasmagoria. But what is truth?

The sun went down behind the variously colored houses in the park. The elegantly dressed residents spilled out from them. Most of these suburban dwellers, these charming lovers of nature, drove along the noisy avenue to the brilliantly illuminated theater that attracted them with a new French light comedy. The evening renewed the usual everyday movement. What had happened yesterday repeated itself monotonously and inexhaustably in Petrovsky Park, just as it did in the heavens where, against a flaming sunset, a white moon rose and Arcturus glimmered, still only barely visible.

In Vera Vladimirovna's drawing room, a very lively and interesting conversation was in progress. Along with a few women friends, among whom Madame Valitskaia maintained first place (so skillfully and artfully had she known how to hide her brilliant matchmaking), Vera Vladimirovna was occupied with the chief concern of her maternal heart: Cecily's imminent wedding. She was seeking friendly advice concerning the wedding dress and the precious stones sent by the jeweler, which were spread out on the table in front of her. She needed to choose those that were the most becoming to the bride.

"I have given her the best part of my own diamonds for her wedding, and they reworked them very tastefully," she said. "But I don't know what to decide on for the other ensemble. Turquoise does not suit her at all."

"These amethysts are very good and the work is excellent," one lady remarked. "But amethysts, however good they are, never produce an effect."

"Choose opals," another lady proposed. "In my opinion, they're the best stones."

"No," Madame Valitskaia exclaimed, "if you wear opals, then they should be unusually fine and priced for a tsar. I would take emeralds; they go wonderfully with black hair and fair skin like Cecily's."

"I would prefer them myself; they are indeed very good on her," Vera Vladimirovna said. "But if this is so, then I will take the set that they brought yesterday. It's incomparably better than this one. These stones are fairly ordinary. They would lose a lot by comparison with Sofia Chardet's emeralds, and I don't want that. Have you seen them?" she added, turning to one of the ladies present.

"Yes," this person answered. "The young lady wore them two days ago at her aunt's soirée. They are amazingly good, especially the bracelets and buttons, and that necklace went superbly with her pale yellow dress."

"She dresses beautifully," another lady said.

"Especially since she married a moneybags," added a third, smiling. Vera Vladimirovna also smiled.

Then she said very seriously, "I cannot fathom how one can sacrifice one's daughter for money in this way. I do not believe that a mother's duty lies in acquiring a rich son-in-law. I understand it differently and in a higher sense. Every mother has a holy responsibility placed upon her, and she is guilty if she does not prefer her daughter's happiness to all other calculations and advantages."

"You do not merely content yourself with defining a mother's duty beautifully," Natalia Afanasevna answered her, deeply touched, "you fulfill this duty even more beautifully, a much rarer thing."

"I can at least bear witness," Vera Vladimirovna continued, conscientiously and modestly, "that my words and deeds are in harmony with each other. I have always proclaimed my convictions sincerely and have always acted in keeping with them."

While these deliberations were going on, Cecily was sitting some distance away with Dmitry and listening only to his quiet words, spoken almost into her ear as if they were a secret, although there was no secret at all to them. The commonplaces that he confided to her in this fashion could have been proclaimed anywhere at all and announced to the whole world; but all these empty speeches seemed to her, of course, interesting in the extreme. After all, it wasn't a matter of what was said. It was the magnetism of a glance, a smile, a voice that was effective here. Meaning was hidden in a thousand imperceptible details. This amorous whispering, this intricate conversation, was of course sensible and proper to the utmost degree. But no matter how well the young couple observed the rules of good society, no matter how decorous Dmitry was, no matter how superbly Cecily had been brought up, they still could not act like complete puppets, and between themselves, they concealed continual transgressions of society's strict laws from Vera Vladimirovna's gaze. And all this was being done so secretly that it resembled a sinful act and was all the sweeter for that.

And what maidenly soul does not understand the charm of these slight transgressions? What woman, making a confession to herself, has not admitted that to touch these heartfelt, troubling joys on the sly, casually, with fear and trembling, is a hundred times more intoxicating than to taste them openly and calmly? And that we, daughters of Eve, all share more or less the opinion of that Italian countess who, eating some delicious ice cream on a torrid day, exclaimed sincerely, "Ah, what a shame that this is not a sin!"

Cecily got up from where she was sitting and went out onto the balcony. Dmitry soon followed her, and they found themselves almost alone. Two thick orange trees whose countless blossoms smelled sweeter toward night separated them from the drawing room and concealed them. Twilight was already closing in; distant stars began to shine brightly, one after another. There were no other witnesses, and Dmitry understood that under God's heaven with the stars watching, it was not shameful to abandon himself to the movement of his heart; he quickly clasped his lovely fiancée and pressed his lips boldly to her pale cheek. . . . She shuddered and tore herself away . . . and then remained motionless, leaning against the glass door. Something had awakened in her and had begun to shine brighter than those stars of the night. Through all the mental veils, through all the ignorance, through all the falsehood of her life shone a gleam of heavenly truth, a sincere feeling, a revelation of the soul . . . a minute flowed by, perhaps unique in her earthly existence . . . and she quietly went back into the drawing room and sat down, lost in thought.

The conversation around the table continued. Cecily listened to the chatter without penetrating its meaning and answered appropriately to questions that she had not understood, with that strange aptitude that we sometimes possess or, more precisely, that possesses us at times when our hearts are sleepwalking. Finally, all the visiting ladies dispersed, Dmitry left too, and Vera Vladimirovna remained alone with her daughter. She took advantage of what was left of the evening to inspect and choose fine lace with Cecily, and incidentally to give her a multitude of moral precepts and useful pieces of advice. Then she made the sign of the cross over her and sent her off to bed. Cecily was impatiently awaiting this opportunity to be alone; she hastened to undress and sent the maid away.

Alone with herself, she leaned her elbows on the soft pillows and submitted to her blissful reveries. An intoxicatingly imperious calm took possession of her soul. *Unhappiness* was a meaningless word for her. She reigned over fate. She was standing before life like a creditor before a debtor, with the right to claim his property. She daringly and fearlessly believed in the unknown future, and in her heart, and in the heart of another. A strange, eternally new, eternally inexplicable phenomenon! What is the reason for striving so joyfully toward the unknown, for committing oneself so blindly? Where is the pledge, where the guarantee? In truth, it is only that unnatural conviction, insane and always deceived. It is the same majestic madness of Don Quixote, who orders a convoy of guards to free the convicts and deliver them to the justice of heaven. He is right, the inspired mad-man, when he trustingly takes the chains off the criminal, and only the depravity of others makes him wrong and comical.

Great souls always preserve this faith in humanity; but everyone has felt it in himself, if only for a few moments.

As children, we've all been told about one excellent trait of Alex-ander the Great. Give us time and we will all, if only once in our lives, stand equal to him; we will all, as he did, drink from the cup, though the whole world has assured us it is poisoned.

And she continued her sweet imaginings, this happy young girl. Already, her thoughts were covered in mist and her dreams wandered, confused by drowsiness; but the bliss in her soul shone through, even though she was half asleep. Her head bent slowly and touched the pillow . . . her long lashes closed . . . and sweetly fall-ing asleep, she suddenly shuddered as in unexpected fright; her eyes shone and again went dark. And the moon came up high and looked in the window . . . and in a sudden burst, from afar, through space something rushed in stormy flight, and the sleepy treetops began to rustle in the darkness, and again fell silent, scarcely breathing. . . .

All is silent; only the fountain's tears
Are falling unseen in the dark of the avenue of trees;
The leaves are sleeping, the vines are still,
The quiet grows more motionless and silent.

What is heard suddenly in the stillness of the night,
Quarrelling with the peacefulness?
Are the hollow depths of the sea rumbling?
Is a thunderstorm murmuring in the distance?

Whose is that nameless and mighty call?
The moon looks from on high into her eyes,
The vale is peaceful, and the heavens without clouds.
Why is her soul full of dread?

He's waiting there, where like a mute shadow
The darkened cypress stands motionless:
They met with a light step,
Silently took each other's hand.

Dim understanding awakened in her,
A prophetic voice filled her heart;
And, leaning into his embrace,
Suddenly her tears poured forth.

What life-giving force flowed
Over her among the wonders of the night?
Whose thought began to speak over her,
Floating into the bottomless heaven?

Was it not his? . . . Hasn't her heart begun to throb
In mutual feeling, like a string?
Wasn't it with his harmonious hymn
That the fountains, and the stars and she could sing?

The time has come! . . . her soul is ready! . . . .
Come to her lips, holy sound! . . .
Crowd into a mysterious word,
A dream of all that is lofty!

Love, incomprehensible miracle!
How do you slip into fragile hearts,
Bright guest, from a place
Where there is no beginning and no end?

Love, entering the corporeal world,
You are made a slave to fate,
You have no heavenly protection,
You have no help from above!

You will not smash the rules made by the crowd,
You will not conquer its passions;
And you will be forever in the wrong,
Forever powerless before it.

A blessed dream of the earthly realm,
You will drift in the fog of life,
Familiar, but always alien,
Always inaccessible to Earth.

The heart will strive in vain
To embody you, sacred rite.
O, cherub, flown down from heaven,
You will return to heaven again!

But your soul has touched divinity,
Its secrets have found a tongue,
Infinity has been thrown open,
And your glance has penetrated the other world.

Send now for a moment, O, spirit of the universe,
Brilliant among those shining worlds,
Boundlessness into perishable form,
Heavenly light into earthly dust!

For a moment, temper trembling souls
In sacred powers;
May eyes gaze and ears hearken,
And earthly murmurs cease!

09

When finally she had managed to arrange properly everything necessary for Cecily's marriage, Vera Vladimirovna set the date of the wedding and consequently left the Park and returned with her daughter to her house on Tverskoi Boulevard. Meanwhile, Dmitry Ivachinsky visited his invalid father in order to receive his blessing and, as far as possible, to prepare his modest dwelling there for Cecily's arrival. She had expressed the desire to spend in rustic solitude those first days of marriage with him, when newlyweds in love cannot get their fill of contemplating one another and fall into happy delusions, imagining that all the rest of the world had been created without need and purpose.

Dmitry was absent for a week, and in the course of that week, he wrote seven long letters to Cecily. Vera Vladimirovna, through whose hands they passed, confiscated two of them. According to her strict, autocratic censorship regulations, she had found in them a certain improper whiff of George-Sandism, which it was necessary to keep from her daughter right up to the wedding itself. Perhaps she was right, but the results of her watchfulness were two sleepless nights for Cecily, in which she racked her brains until morning about the possible content of these two hidden letters, tirelessly thinking up countless solutions to this interesting riddle.

Finally, after this endless, seven-day absence, Dmitry returned, more in love than ever. He was one of those people who in all their feelings and actions seem to be walking along a steep, downhill slope. They lack the strength to stop for a minute, and with each step, they get more and more carried away. Like all of them, Dmitry took this insufficiency of strength for fervency of character and insuperable storminess of passion. The reunion was touching. Vera Vladimirovna herself was deeply moved on this occasion and was convinced of the future happiness of her Cecily, about which all the people she knew (and even those she didn't know) were speaking with much sympathetic interest.

The long-awaited hour drew near and at last arrived. On the eve of the day that was supposed so happily to change her entire life, the bride was sitting at the window of her room and gazing in quiet contemplation at the long boulevard. It was the beginning of the second half of August, a month almost always autumnal in Russia. The day was overcast; cold, bluish-gray clouds drifted lazily across the heavens. Moscow still preserved its deserted summer appearance. Rarely did a carriage pass along the sedate street. On the empty boulevard, a hurried, plebeian passer-by in a dark-blue caftan or a gray peasant's coat would appear from time to time. The dusty lime trees stood motionless, with a sort of tired, bored expression. The humid air promised rain.

What was Cecily thinking about for so long, with such a distracted look? What was the cause of this almost-despondent daydreaming? She herself could not have said. We are powerless before our own incomprehensible feelings, and our impressions do not depend on any external events. Who has not sometimes felt weighed down and sad at heart in the midst of splendid festivity, of general noisy gaiety and their own happiness? Perhaps she was experiencing at that moment how strangely sometimes a person's heart fears the imminent fulfillment of passionate desires, as if she understands, though only for an instant, all the blindness and insignificance.

The entrance of the maid Annushka interrupted this wayward meditation.

"Your mother kindly requests that you go down to dine; she is already at table."

"What," Cecily said, "is it really so late?"

"It's after five, miss."

Cecily hurried to the dining room, where her mother was waiting for her.

Dmitry was not there that day.

Vera Vladimirovna wanted Cecily to spend this evening alone with her girlfriends in something like the traditional maiden's party.

Vera Vladimirovna was well known for her patriotism and love for all Russian customs, although when she happened to observe them, she gave them a rather French look. After eight, Cecily's young friends came to visit. First to arrive, unusually merry, was Olga. For the last few days, Prince Victor had been extraordinarily courteous toward her, as she lost no time telling Cecily when they were alone.

"Imagine, darling, yesterday I was in a frightful situation. You know we had a large cavalcade to Pokrovskoe arranged for yesterday. That marvelous traveler whom you saw at our house, Lord Granville, took part in it and made me a bet that he would overtake me. I agreed to the bet, trusting in the speed of my horse. But that morning, they suddenly came and told me that the horse was lame. This happened in the presence of Prince Victor, who had dropped in to inquire about Mother's health. I was in despair that I would have to refuse to take part in the cavalcade, and especially that I would have to refuse the bet with milord. Meanwhile, Prince Victor had left and, imagine, an hour later, he sent me his groom with Gulnara, his best horse, and told him to tell me that he sincerely wished that I would win my bet riding her. I did win, indeed! How do you like that?"

Cecily shared with all her heart in Olga's happiness.

"I always thought," she said, "that you would be the wife of Prince Victor. May God grant you happiness!"

Olga threw herself into Cecily's arms. The other visitors entered, and the usual conversation of young girls began: happy chatter, light mockery of absent friends, innocent secrets whispered in the ear, sometimes by chance a caustic word—and all of this was surprisingly graceful.

Cecily, of course, was the *tsaritsa* of the enchanting circle: her friends were paying that involuntary tribute that belongs by right to the triumphant one chosen in love. All these shrewd, uninitiated Ondines understand this. She herself radiated the sweet pride that every bride feels in herself, even the poor bride-to-be of a craftsman. Her vague morning thoughts had completely disappeared. Once again, she trusted joyfully in her fate. The young guests were busy with the presents given her by her fiancé, mother, and relatives. They inspected, interrogated, praised, evaluated, envied—and the hours went by in a merry and lively fashion.

They were passing even more merrily at that same time in the drawing room of a house near the Arbat gates, where Dmitry Ivachinsky lived. That evening, during a boisterous conversation with ten or so friends, he was bidding farewell to his bachelor existence. Champagne was flowing, and the smoke of cigars was rising around the table where dinner had ended a little while before. On the tablecloth, bottles crowded together, goblets sparkled, and large, dark spots of spilled burgundy and Lafitte appeared. The young rakes were entering into a euphoric state. Shouts, arguments, gales of laughter, pointed jokes, and the whole concoction of crude masculine entertainment resounded. Ilichev was telling indecent jokes. His audience laughed at the top of their voices. Dmitry laughed loudest of all; he also overdid merrymaking, just as he did sensitivity and sadness. He always feared being unable to justify to himself the respect he had for his own unbridled strength.

Meanwhile, Cecily was speaking to her circle of friends about the unbelievable meekness and timidity of her future husband's love and was enumerating all his virtues. It was already quite late. The young girls went out onto the balcony. The starry sky sparkled; the dark clouds of the morning had moved away and lay in a black band along the horizon. Cecily leaned against the railing and remembered standing with the same friends on the same balcony on a May night three months earlier, and she thought with heartfelt pleasure how much had come to pass for her—how happily her fate had changed in these three months.

When all the merry guests had left, when Cecily had wished her mother good night and gone into her bedroom, she was filled with joyful agitation. In the course of the whole evening, she had spoken with her friends so much about Dmitry, had so recalled and praised all his merits and fine qualities, so boasted of his love and her own happiness that, drunk with the sweet intoxication of this conversation, she found herself still under the pleasant influence of her own words. She rang for the maid, freed her long braids, unwound her constricting sash, threw off her dress and her tight corset, shook off her graceful shoes with a light movement and, putting on a comfortable peignoir and slipping her bare feet into soft Turkish slippers, she sent Annushka away and sat down on the sofa. The door closed after the maid. Silence and peaceful twilight surrounded the young bride-to-be. The cozy bedroom was lit only by the icon lamp, weakly and mysteriously shining from its high frame. The languid ray of light fell on her bowed head with its loosened black hair, the pure brow, the sweet half-smile of the tender dreamer. Her young soul was telling itself some silent, wonderful tale in the silence of the night. The stars glimmered through the long, muslin curtains on the windows of the quiet room.

In Dmitry's room, the noise increased. The champagne was replaced by rum; in the middle of the table, hot punch floated with a blue flame as the orgy descended into complete debauchery. Two or three of the more feeble types were already lying on sofas, but the remaining heroes were shouting and laughing all the louder, although a bit senselessly.

"Ivachinsky!" yelled Ilichev, "is it because you really are taking leave of the joys of life that you're drinking with such desperation?"

"I see now that you're drunk," Dmitry answered, "because you're beginning to utter absurdities."

"Gentlemen," Ilichev continued in a loud voice, raising his full glass, "I drink to Ivachinsky's health, and I wager that from tomorrow on, he'll become a most moral person and a virtuous family man. He'll take a stroll along the boulevard with his wife on his arm, drink only blameless tea, and later boiled milk with his children."

The din of laughter sounded anew.

"Do you hear that, Ivachinsky?" some voices cried out.

"I do."

"Well, aren't you answering?"

"What should I answer to such nonsense?"

"You see, Ivachinsky," Ilichev said, "what a fine reputation you have. They all agree with me, and no one wants to take up my bet."

Of all the soul's impressions, shame is the most conventional and the one most capable of being falsely applied. Dmitry felt ashamed that these wastrels could assume him capable of settling down. Most likely, in the company of a brazen thief, he would have been ashamed that he did not steal.

"I'll take your bet," he cried out, "and, in a week from today, I'll invite you all to a heroic drinking bout with the gypsies."

"Bravo!" the guests cried noisily. "It's a deal!"

"Of course," one of them added, "who would want to get married if the blessed state of matrimony made it necessary to give up wine and good times!"

"He's bragging," Ilichev said. "Look at him! What if his wife were to find out!"

Dmitry waved his arm with inexpressibly heroic scorn and immediately drank down his glass of hot punch to the dregs.

In her quiet bedroom, Cecily was still sitting in profound meditation, but little by little, her dreams were changing unaccountably. She looked around her at this modest, chaste room that tomorrow she would have to leave forever, and at that moment, she dimly understood a great deal. All her childish, bright peacefulness, so proudly scorned, suddenly flashed before her like a priceless but lost treasure. A weight lay on her heart. She tried to console herself by enumerating yet again all Dmitry's virtues, all the guarantees of her future happiness, but now they somehow failed to come to mind. A senseless fear and a mysterious grief gripped her soul ever more painfully. Her nerves were severely strained. She didn't have the strength to throw off this oppressive thought from her heart. She sat with bowed head, mute under the weight of this inexplicable feeling. Suddenly, a shudder ran through her, and she remained motionless as in a trance. As Cecily leaned slightly forward, strangely staring into the twilight, with inexpressible sadness in her face, through walls and through space, it was as if she had reached that boisterous festivity, as if she could see the piercing flame of the hot punch and hear the sharp laughter of a familiar voice.

Finally, she stood up weakly, went to the corner where the icon gleamed in its golden frame, and fell to her knees with a heavy sigh before the holy countenance that looked so peacefully at all the heart's storms, at all earthly woe.

She lay for a long time before the icon, trying in vain to gain control of her thoughts, in bitter reverie, not praying—if grief and humility are not a prayer. Then, somewhat eased, she got up, went to her bed, and lay down for the last time on that peaceful, maidenly bed where for so many nights she had dreamed so sweetly, slept so quietly. Her pale brow sank onto the pillows. She lay for some time stretched out like a marble effigy on a tomb.

The ornate clock in the small column between the windows struck one sonorous chime in the silence of night. Cecily slowly raised herself up and looked. She had remembered something and couldn't recall it clearly, some word that she couldn't find, some name that didn't come to her. . . . And she felt and knew that everything going on now had definitely already happened to her once, that this moment was a repetition of something in her past and that she had already lived through it once before. . . . "My God!" she whispered almost aloud, "who has died? . . . What is this? . . ."

She struggled with sleep.

But her whole soul was gradually filled with a timid, sweetly sad expectation, a nebulous desire, like another, unfathomable love. Slowly, soft, bright tears slid from her dark, lowered eyelashes. She was falling asleep like a hurt, half-soothed child. . . . And now she remembered . . . there was hush all around. . . . Wasn't it time? . . . She was alone . . . what was going to happen? . . .

> The stars shine menacingly above her,
> The night is infinite, the valley barely visible;
> She is alone . . . perhaps it is too late,
> Perhaps the time of encounter has passed.

> The midnight bird has taken wing . . .
> The earth is silent like the grave;
> From time to time the angry summer lightning
> Flashes in the dusky distance.

> And suddenly he stands beside her,
> Lowering his gloomy brow,
> Unmoving, with a hopeless look,
> In heavy, silent meditation.

> "You have come again! . . . and are we not in a dream? . . .
> Why was our path so separate? . . .
> Why are your lips so silent? . . .
> Why is terror descending on my heart? . . ."

And he bent over, pale and grieving,
And he offered words of sadness:
"Let us say farewell today, my poor friend:
Let life claim its rights!

Go back to the realm of Earth,
Go to your earthly triumph—
I yield you over to the world,
With an anxious prayer to the Creator.

Sorrow has He given to all of us equally,
To all a measure of sad days;
Submit to His laws
The murmur of your pride.

Learn to live in outward agitation,
Forgetting the Eden of youthful dreams,
Share no more with anyone
The secret of inconsolable meditation.

Not in vain did your heart's fantasies
Strive so eagerly toward existence,
Life will mercilessly fulfill
Your passionate request.

And the bright glow
Of enchanted mist will dissipate;
Too late, too soon,
You will know the gift you have awaited.

And fate will more than carry out
Its sentence over you:
But you will not lie down in cruel torment,
You will not fall in battle.

You will find amid the struggles
Of years illusionless and hard,
Many pure distractions,
Many joyful victories.

You will bear the insults of your friends,
The evil lies of angry words—
And you will raise the veil
From the mysterious goddess Isis.

You will understand earthly reality
With a maturing soul:
You will buy a dear blessing
At a dear price.

You will calm your heart's hostility,
You will not avert your eyes from misfortune,
Neither moments of deception nor of hope
Will trouble you.

All that is today unconscious
Alien to all, will flower in you—
The burning agony of life
Will turn into rich fruit.

So, go as you've been sentenced,
Strong in faith only,
Not hoping for support,
Defenseless and alone.

Don't disturb the heavens, transgressing,
Silence your own dreams.
And dare to ask of God
Only your daily bread."

10

T he next day, after seven in the evening, Vera Vladimirov-
na's magnificently illuminated and decorated house glit-
tered in the darkening twilight. People thronged Tverskoi
Boulevard opposite the bright windows and, as usual, admired good-
heartedly the arrogant luxury and unattainable happiness of the rich.
In a luxurious private room, in front of a huge mirror lit with the
bright light of candelabras, surrounded by her young friends, Cec-
ily was putting on that beautiful, solemn dress that all those pretty
little heads dreamed about, the specter of which so captivatingly and
persistently arises in maidenly reveries; and even poor Nadezhda
Ivanovna, bustling about the bride, still had not despaired of array-
ing herself in it.

And the bride looked inexpressibly lovely in that wedding attire,
with its wonderful veil falling transparently onto her young shoul-
ders, with those white orange blossoms trembling brightly in the
black of her curls, with those sparkling diamonds, with that pale face,
with those thoughtful eyes.

Cecily was feeling nervous, as is natural at such a moment, and
was not able to understand her mysterious inner feelings. It seemed
to her at times that she was in a dream, that in fact she was not being

taken to the church to get married, and she asked herself: How did all this come about so soon? How is it that I am marrying Dmitry?

Her apparel was complete. They handed her one more gorgeous bracelet, a gift from the groom. She stretched out her arm so they could put it on her and, looking with a distracted gaze at Olga while she fastened the lock, Cecily whispered deep in thought:

> So, go as you've been sentenced,
> Defenseless and alone. . . .

"What are you saying?" Olga asked, looking at her with surprise.

"I don't know," Cecily answered. "It's some song that has been going round in my head. I can't remember where I heard it."

"What nonsense!" Olga said. "Go on, you're ready. Put on your gloves. It's time to go."

An hour later near the Arbat gates, at the wealthy parish church of the Apparition of St. Nicholas, smart carriages were lining up in a long row. The church was bright with candlelight. Aristocratic society was crowded together inside it and in the doorway a plebeian crowd gaped at the wedding, jostling intensely in an attempt to catch a glimpse of the handsome couple from afar.

Cecily stood pale, with head quietly bowed beneath the heavy crown whose burden, perhaps symbolic, she seemed to feel on her young brow.[1] Her limbs trembled slightly and her glance flew up anxiously two or three times along the iconostasis to the top of the cupola, where the rainy sky shone black through a high window.

---

1. In the Orthodox wedding ceremony, heavy crowns are held over (rather than placed on) the heads of the bride and groom for part of the service.

Among the spectators near the doors the usual chatter and comments, questions and answers proceeded in half-whispers.

"What's she looking so serious for? Don't she want to get married?"

"No, it's for love."

"Look at those diamonds!"

"So, then, he's rich?"

"They say he's poor."

"He's good-looking, though."

"Pardon me," a friend standing with Ilichev in a corner of the church said, "How can she be called a beauty? She's not at all pretty. She's pale as a corpse."

"She's sick with nerves," Ilichev answered.

"Hah!" the other continued, "these nervous wives are a punishment from God! Life with her will be no joy for him."

"He'll cure her," Ilichev said cold-bloodedly.

The solemn ceremony came to an end. Relatives, friends and acquaintances surrounded the young pair, congratulating them and accompanying them to the porch of the church. At the exit, Prince Victor went up to Madame Valitskaia with his stiff, barely noticeable bow.

"I don't suppose you have any errands to give me in Paris?" he said to her casually. "I'm leaving tomorrow."

"What?" the frightened Natalia Afanasevna asked. "You are going? I hope not for long."

"I don't know," the prince answered. "Probably for long."

Natalia Afanasevna found the strength almost to smile and utter a few words in which were included, not altogether clearly, the wish for a happy journey. The prince bowed slightly again and disappeared along with all her fine hopes.

Why ever had she, poor woman, so diligently striven and so skill-fully married off Cecily to Ivachinsky? All her expertise had been in vain; all her labors had come to nothing.

She bit her lip and followed the others out.

Vera Vladimirovna, standing on the porch of the church, wiped her eyes, full of tears of joy.

The carriages were brought round, the clatter of wheels resounded, the clip-clop of the horses, the cry of the postilions, the shouts of the coachmen and lackeys—the whole loud hubbub of departure. The people dispersed. The lights in the church were extinguished.

Soon afterward, the church stood dark and mute on the wide empty street. Above it, heavy, menacing clouds went slowly by and were carried away to no one knows where.

Cherished thought has claimed what was its own,
Found speech, crossed over to the outer world.
Long had it lived mid worldly noise,
Free and bright within me.

And I was able in my soul to keep
A portion silently for myself alone,
And now I look upon my cause
With an involuntary and strange sadness.

And then it occurs to me again
That it's time for me to meet life differently,
That dreams are lies, the word is useless,
Sound and verse an empty game.

This is, perhaps, the final song:
Dreams fly away faster than the years!
Shall I too recognize the vain power of the world?
Shall I too forget the service of beauty?

Now you have warmed my soul's depths for the first time
Will you bid me farewell, poetry?
Will I abandon you, youthful beliefs?
Will I find meaningless peace?

Having known the joys and sorrows of the Earth,
Having lived through the anxious years,
Will I say, as many have said:
All is empty fantasy! All is sad vanity!

My spirit weakens and the goal is far off.
The crazy hope of yesterday
Is scarce remembered and the voice of self-reproach
Rings louder and more threatening in my heart.

I am oppressed with impotent searching,
I am full of burdensome questions.
Consciousness alone lives in my soul,
The only strength, and may it never die!

Then let the future threaten loss,
And the heart's dreams grow thinner every day;
Let me pay a woeful price
For the bright gifts of my youth;

Though I throw treasure after treasure
Into the stormy depths of the sea of life:
Blessed the one who, arguing with the storm,
Can salvage something precious.

Written between 1844 and 1847

AFTERWORD

Karolina Pavlova: Translator and Writer

DANIEL GREEN

T he creative work of translators is often overlooked, yet a skillful translation can set different cultures and times in conversation with each other. Barbara Heldt's 1978 English rendering of Karolina Pavlova's *A Double Life*, presented here in its fourth edition, offers a striking example of how a translation can play a role in changing the way academia, and the reading public more broadly, thinks about a particular literary tradition. Although Pavlova achieved significant recognition in her lifetime for her poetic talent, rubbed shoulders with some of the great names of Russian literature's Golden Age (including Pushkin, Lermontov, and Gogol), and later inspired the Symbolist poets of the Silver Age, she has had long periods of relative obscurity. *A Double Life* appeared just once as a stand-alone book in Russian: at the time of its first publication in 1848. Since then, it has appeared only in collected works, the most recent of which dates back to 1964.[1] It has not been in print in Russian since then. In contrast, Heldt's translation, along with a slow but steady stream of scholarship on Pavlova, has kept *A Double Life* and its author in the mind of the anglophone reader for the last four decades.

This translation of *A Double Life* has been part of a fundamental transformation in how the English-speaking world sees Russian literature, driven by what has been called the "rediscovery" or "recovery" of nineteenth-century women writers. For much of the twentieth century, even women whose works had achieved significant readerships and recognition in their lifetimes were largely written out of literary histories and their works were little published. Heldt and others threw down the gauntlet and challenged readers to reimagine the Russian literary canon as something that included a wider variety of voices than just the "great men" whose names are still most familiar to audiences today. In doing so, they sought both to better reflect the range of Russian literature as it was produced and read and to uncover the cultural processes that privileged certain types of writing and literature by certain kinds of people over others.

From a practical standpoint, this translation of *A Double Life* finally made it possible for teachers to include a nineteenth-century female writer on syllabi for Russian literature courses in translation. As a result, for the first time in an English-language context, Pavlova was able to stand on equal footing in university courses with her better-known male contemporaries. A wave of translations of women writers followed. *A Double Life* now sits on the bookshelf alongside a growing number of texts by nineteenth-century Russian women in English, including titles in the Russian Library series.

The practice of translating women writers coincided with scholarly reappraisals of Russian literature as a space in which questions of gender were reflected and played out. Heldt's own *Terrible Perfection: Women and Russian Literature* (Bloomington: Indiana University Press, 1987) provided the first substantial critique of the male-dominated Russian canon. It was followed a few years later by two other pioneering works: Catriona Kelly's *History of Russian Women Writers* (Oxford: Oxford University Press, 1994) and the *Dictionary of Russian Women Writers* by Marina Ledkovsky, Charlotte Rosenthal, and Mary Zirin (Westport, CT: Greenwood Press, 1994). These significantly fleshed out the contextual landscape of female writing, whose relationship and interconnection with the dominant male literature of the time has since been explored by Jehanne Gheith and others.[2]

NEW KINDS OF SCHOLARSHIP

With the rediscovery of writing by women and the changing understanding of who was writing in nineteenth-century Russia came a recognition of the need for new scholarly approaches. Toward the end of the twentieth century, scholars were already paying more attention to the social and economic circumstances in which works were produced. This approach proved extremely important for the study of women writers, whose status within society informed not only how they wrote and published but also what they wrote about.

Modern writing on gender differs from that of the nineteenth-century critics in its move away from essentializing female writing, which is to say, finding something innately female in the way women write. Since Judith Butler's 1988 essay "Performative Acts and Gender Constitution," the notion of gender as something performed rather than inherent has informed our understanding not only of how women present their writing but also of how they navigate social and literary norms. A feminist reading requires a reanalysis of literary institutions—from the salon to the journal to the critical response—and a new understanding of genre—the conventional forms a work takes. The result is to read female writing on its own terms, rather than as a poor relation to the mainstream male tradition, but not to separate it from the male-dominated culture in which it was produced.

This approach suits *A Double Life* very well, uncovering how the themes of the story are connected with how it was produced and read. While it would be a mistake to assign to Pavlova modern feminist critical views on the structures of society, we may still read the text and Pavlova's life through that lens. That it is natural for us to do so is a testament not only to Heldt's work as a translator and scholar but also to changes in the field of Russian studies that she and others helped bring about. When reading this English translation of *A Double Life*, we are thus engaging with a cultural product of both the 1840s and the 1970s that helped to define how writing by women was to be read.

CRITICAL RESPONSES TO *A DOUBLE LIFE*

By the late 1840s Pavlova had seen her original poetry in print many times. To get to this point, she had followed a well-trodden path available to both men and women: making connections and a name for herself by doing translation work. Her poetry appeared in journals edited by friends whom she had met at various salons, where literary figures could socialize and share their work. *A Double Life*, too, appeared with a press used by others in her circle. Yet its publication was only the first step to her being taken seriously as a writer.

Although many contemporary reviews of *A Double Life* were positive, Pavlova still had to contend with expectations of what female writing should be like. An anonymous critic writing in *The Library for Reading* praised *A Double Life*, but packaged his admiration in gendered language: "I admit that, in the middle of the book, I suddenly had my doubts and looked again at the book's title page to make certain—'did I not make a mistake?—was it really written by a woman? I had somehow thought that only men could be so sharp.' "[3] Others were less positive, such as Baron Rozen, who wrote in the journal *The Son of the Fatherland*:

> Reading a new book for a review, first of all you try to determine its main idea and what exactly the author wanted; this is particularly difficult when the main idea is unclear even to the author, when it moves into mysticism and wanders through the magnetic visions of the soul.[4]

What all the reviewers had in common, though, was an obsession with Pavlova's femininity. Rozen was thus able to dismiss one positive response to *A Double Life* by Pavlova's friend Konstantin Aksakov as "chivalric praise."[5]

In the mid-nineteenth century, Russian criticism was still in its infancy, but its attitude toward women writers had already been established. Women were thought to have a narrower perspective, one that focused inward upon the self. In contrast, men were considered better able to creatively imagine the lives of others.[6] Of course, women were also restricted in the range of experiences open to them; unlike noblemen, noblewomen did not work and could not serve the state in any official capacity.

What would soon become known as the "woman question"—
the discussion of the position of women in society—is an overt
theme of *A Double Life*. The reviewer for the journal *The Contem-
porary* applauds Pavlova for dealing with such a topic. He writes:
"in it the poet touches on extremely important questions, namely
the upbringing of society girls, their position in high society, their
conditional marriages, and finally their adult childhood."[7] The
expression "adult childhood" suggests that women occupy not just a
marginal but even a liminal place in society, stuck in limbo between
the irresponsible status of the children they raise and the full-fledged
agency of true (which is to say, masculine) adulthood. Yet while
the reviewer may ostensibly empathize with the plight of women,
he nonetheless prioritizes not women's experience but how female
behavior might impact men, as the quotation in Heldt's introduction
shows (see page xxiv).

Baron Rozen goes further in his review. Not only is he uninter-
ested in the female social concerns raised by the character of Cec-
ily in *A Double Life*, but he takes her love interest Dmitry's part
and expresses gratitude that the story stops before the reader sees
the difficult life Dmitry will have with Cecily: "and it is very good
that the curtain falls: someone of the likes of Dmitry Ivaginsky
[*sic*] most likely would not cope with such a wife: she will make
things miserable for him!" These acts of sidelining and erasing
female experience demonstrate a lack of ability or will on the part
of the male critics to embrace a female perspective. They go hand
in hand with the restrictions on what were considered accept-
able experiences for women in society as laid out in the story.
For example, Cecily is warned away from contact with poetry by
her mother:

And although, as we have seen, Vera Vladimirovna greatly respected and loved poetry, she still considered it improper for a young girl to spend too much of her time on it. She quite justly feared any development of imagination and inspiration, those eternal enemies of propriety. She molded the spiritual gifts of her daughter so carefully that Cecily, instead of dreaming of the Marquis Poza, of Egmont, of Lara and the like, could only dream of a splendid ball, a new gown, and the outdoor fête on the first of May.

When Cecily is exposed to poetry, though, she cannot help but be inspired. When she goes to bed at night she is free from social expectations, and her poetic sensibilities are given free rein in her dreams. Cecily, in fact, has been warned off just those interests that Pavlova herself possessed and that she harnessed to shine a light on society in *A Double Life*. Vera Vladimirovna is glad that Cecily does not dream about characters in literary works by people who interested Pavlova: Lara is the heroine of an eponymous narrative poem by Byron, with whose poem "Dream" *A Double Life* is in direct dialogue; Egmont is the hero of a play by the same name by Goethe, with whom Pavlova corresponded; and the Marquis Poza is a character from *Don Carlos*, a play by Friedrich Schiller, a writer whose works Pavlova translated. Most dangerous for Cecily in the eyes of her mother is the composition of original artistic works. She is praised instead for her feminine accomplishments of sketching and singing.

One feature that makes *A Double Life* unique is its unusual combination of poetry and prose. Each chapter covers a day's events in the more "realistic" medium of prose, then Cecily's subsequent nighttime dream life is rendered in poetry. No matter how much her creative impulse might be suppressed during the day, it finds an

outlet at night. The move from prose to poetry marks two bound-
aries: between night and day and between a life following social
conventions and one in which Cecily is free to roam creatively. This
idea is echoed in the title, which is taken from Byron's 1816 poem
"Dream," whose first two and a half lines are given as the epigraph
to the story:

> Our life is twofold; Sleep hath its own world,
> A boundary between the things misnamed
> Death and existence

The reader is prompted to ask whether the "real" Cecily is the one
who wears ball gowns and falls in love with inappropriate men dur-
ing the day or the one who dreams in poetry at night. The quotation
also raises the question of whether sleep or a life of conventions is
most akin to death.

While critics were mostly impressed by the inclusion of poetic
interludes, another genre question puzzled them: Pavlova's choice to
subtitle the story a "sketch" ("*ocherk*" in Russian). The term "sketch"
brings to mind the "physiological sketch," which had its origins in
France. These introduced the reading public to a variety of "types"
of people from the lower classes whom the reader might not have
examined closely otherwise. In an introduction to *The Physiology of
Petersburg*, a celebrated almanac of Russian physiological sketches
edited by Nikolai Nekrasov, the critic Vissarion Belinsky character-
izes the sketch as a genre that places greater emphasis on observa-
tion and mimetic accuracy than on literary quality.[8] Pavlova's version
is thus unusual in its length, literary quality, and focus on a highborn
subject in the form of Cecily.

Pavlova used the genre designation of "sketch" to suggest that the Russian noblewoman was just as deserving of scrutiny and pity as a poor Russian man on the street.[9] However, Pavlova's version of the sketch goes far beyond the genre's ordinary confines, asking the reader not only to pity Cecily but also to understand her and the world of which she is a part. Just as Cecily struggles against social strictures, *A Double Life* oversteps the boundaries of the sketch genre. Cecily pushes against the banal life set out for her by society and the story pushes against the bland norms of the genre, bringing the life of a young girl on the marriage market into the realm of rich narrative prose and poetry. In doing so, Pavlova turns the sketch into something more inclusive of a female perspective and more penetrating into the inner life of its main protagonist.

Pavlova puts Cecily's feelings at the heart of the story and adds to them the experiences of a widening circle of female voices from the narrator to her imagined readers. For example, the reader is invited to share the narrator's recognition of the delights of Cecily's romantic infatuation:

> What woman, making a confession to herself, has not admitted that to touch these heartfelt, troubling joys on the sly, casually, with fear and trembling, is a hundred times more intoxicating than to taste them openly and calmly? And that we, daughters of Eve, all share more or less the opinion of that Italian countess who, eating some delicious ice cream on a torrid day, exclaimed sincerely, "Ah, what a shame that this is not a sin!"

That male critics might feel excluded from the "we" of this passage is perhaps not surprising. Yet some were able to see beyond their

differences in gender and grasp the universal experiences of human-
ity in *A Double Life*. For others, however, the perspective of a young
woman was too alien, and thus they felt that it lacked what they
thought of as the more universal perspective of male writers. In read-
ings of Russian literature, this assumption that a male perspective is
the norm against which others are to be measured was not signifi-
cantly challenged until recently.

PAVLOVA AS TRANSLATOR AND SALON HOST

Pavlova, of course, could not know how history would treat her writ-
ing, but she was well aware of the particular challenges she faced as
a female writer in mid-nineteenth-century Russia. One activity that
offered her the possibility of advancement was translation. Yet trans-
lation also reinforced her inferior status as a female interpreter of a
masculine world.

Pavlova's first published volume, *The Northern Lights* (*Das Nor-
dlicht*), which appeared in 1833 under her then surname, Jaenisch,
linked her creative work (producing translations and writing origi-
nal poetry) with that of successful men. In it, Pavlova presented her
German translations of contemporary Russian poetry and a small
amount of prose and appended several original poems of her own.
The poems she translated were by those recognized as Russia's lead-
ing poets of the time, among them Pushkin, Zhukovsky, Iazykov, and
Baratynsky. All of the Russian poets whose works Pavlova translated
into German in *The Northern Lights* were translators themselves.
Indeed, translation was seen as both an important literary endeavor
in its own right and a common means of advancing one's literary

career. For Pavlova it held an additional attraction: translation was considered an acceptable creative activity for women and was certainly more tolerated than writing original works. She had decades of precedents as a female translator: noblewomen, who were often well educated in foreign languages, had been prolific translators since the 1760s. However, they rarely received as much recognition for their work as their male counterparts.[10]

In *The Northern Lights*, Pavlova associates herself with another influential man by addressing one of her poems to the German scientist Alexander von Humboldt, whom she had met a few years previously, and by noting that the suggestion that she produce translations of Russian literature for a German audience had come from him. In her foreword she is careful not to emphasize her creativity and makes no mention of her own poetry. Furthermore, when she writes about her translation work she provides numerous justifications for her project: her qualifications as a translator as well as the reasoning behind how she compiled the volume and made her translation choices in terms of meter and rhyme. We can see the addition of her own original work to the volume as a step toward setting herself on the same level as other writers, yet her poems are included only tentatively, at the end, set apart from what comes before. Unlike the earlier poems, they are presented as poetry written by a translator rather than someone who is a poet in her own right.

By all accounts, Pavlova was right to have low expectations for how much credit she would receive for her creative work. She received little acknowledgment for the volume either in the Russian critical press or from the men whose works she was introducing to a German-speaking audience. Baratynsky, for instance, gave his ignorance of German as an excuse for not showing Pavlova gratitude for translating his poems.[11]

There was an additional factor that contributed to the paucity of socio-literary capital that she gained through her translation work: her choice of language. Pavlova faced the double obstacles to being accepted into literary circles of her gender and her German origins. This disdain toward Germans in society appears on the first page of the story. Ilichev, who also later shows contempt for women by persuading Dmitry to cheat on the heroine of the story, Cecily, here expresses his negative feelings toward her ethnicity, saying: "I can't stand all these Germans and half-Germans." Pavlova, as a Lutheran in Russian Orthodox society, grew up as an outsider in the country of her birth. That her translations did not result in acceptance among her Russian peers also cannot have been helped by the kind of translation she was performing: not *into* Russian but *from* Russian into German and sometimes French.

Whereas translators into Russian produced works that were read and discussed by a circle of acquaintances in Russia, translating a Russian work into a foreign language gave an individual writer a wider international audience, but did not have much impact within Russian society. Russian poets therefore would not have felt the results of Pavlova's translations particularly strongly. It is notable that in her two other big translation projects, which were published six years later, she moved away from Russian poetry as a source of translation material. Her second volume, *The Preludes* (*Les Préludes*), published in French in Paris in 1839, also included her own poetry alongside her translations. What made it different from *The Northern Lights* was not only the language she was translating into but also her choice of what to translate. In *The Preludes* Pavlova includes only a handful of translations from Russian; the rest comprises masterpieces of European writing originally in English, Polish, German, and Italian. The same year, she also published a rendering into French of Schiller's *Maid of Orleans* (*Die Jungfrau von Orleans*) under the title *Joan of Arc* (*Jeanne d'Arc*). It seems that toward the end of the 1830s, Pavlova was less seeking recognition from her fellow Russian poets for her translation work and more a place on the European literary stage.

We can see a similar progression in Pavlova's relationship with Russian literary society in her role as salon host. By the time Pavlova published *A Double Life* in 1848, the salon she ran with her husband was already well established. Salons, particularly two run by women, proved key places where Pavlova could make important literary contacts. She was first introduced into literary high society at Avdotya Elagina's salon. Later, at Zinaida Volkonskaya's, she met, among others, Russia's national poet, Alexander Pushkin, and his exiled Polish counterpart, Adam Mickiewicz, to whom she became engaged before her marriage to Nikolai Pavlov. Once she was married, she became eligible in the eyes of society to run her own literary salon. Yet there, too, male voices were privileged and thus predominated. Ostensibly, in a salon, women and men could meet as equals: both could act as hosts. However, female roles were also limited by gender expectations. Female hosts were expected to be an audience, critic, and muse for male guests. Pavlova, in contrast, broke the mold and presented her own work to her guests, something that provoked stinging criticism from some quarters.[12]

The job of the translator and that of a salon host are not entirely dissimilar. Just as a skillfully orchestrated salon brings together talented people of varying artistic and intellectual backgrounds, the thoughtfully rendered translation unites the styles and worldviews of two different cultures. Pavlova was excellent in both these roles deemed acceptable by the gender conventions of her day. She received pushback from her peers, however, when she strayed outside others' expectations and asserted her right to employ her talents to act and write as she wished.

CONCLUSION

Translation was entwined with questions of creativity and gender both in how Pavlova came to write and publish *A Double Life* and in how we have the story today in Heldt's translation. Translation also gives us a way to consider gender in the story: just as Heldt had to consider how to render Pavlova's Russian text in a way that is accessible to the modern English-speaking reader, Pavlova was faced with the question of how to present the particular experiences of a marriageable young Russian woman to a readership that was reluctant to take such a perspective seriously.

The complexity of this challenge can be seen in the relationship between the prosaic and poetic elements in the text. There is an irony in the liberation Cecily experiences in the poetry, which is a form regulated by rhyme and meter. To this we can add another set of considerations when looking at the translation into English. Heldt renders the poetic sections of *A Double Life* without regard for the original rhyme or rhythm, choosing instead to prioritize another important feature of poetry: the imagery. This is an excellent example of the translator's talent for cultural matchmaking. Not only does it make these sections sound more natural to the modern English ear (rhyme being far more common in the Russian tradition), but it also makes them feel more relevant to readers today. By choosing to render the poetry without rhyme, Heldt anticipates her readers' cultural context, making it possible for them to engage more directly with a work from a very different time and place.

The transformative power of translation can also be seen directly within the story of *A Double Life*. The poetry that first sets Cecily's imagination ablaze is not an original work but a translation of Schiller's 1799 poem "The Song of the Bell" ("Das Lied von der Glocke") read out as part of an evening's entertainment. Yet although Cecily is fascinated, the narrative focuses on the boredom of the audience. The majority of the soirée's attendees are indifferent to the poem and unappreciative of the translation work of the poet. Where they manage to find a compliment, it is delivered in a condescending manner, as demonstrated in the exchange below:

> One lady among the charming neighbors of the man of letters leaned close to him and asked sympathetically, "How long did this marvelous translation take you?"
>
> "I don't know," answered the poor confused young man.
>
> She turned away with a barely perceptible smile.

A subsequent conversation about the purpose of poetry takes place without once involving the poet-translator. The audience is also particularly adept at not engaging with the poetry itself: alongside their empty praise, people criticize its length and its lack of usefulness and contemporaneity. The reader is drawn along with the rest of the gathering, experiencing the reading through the perspective of the high-society crowd. Like any other member of the audience, the reader initially accepts the norms of reception before the feelings of the poet provide a contrast. The reader is thus challenged to engage in the same struggle as Cecily: deciding whether to follow social norms or to break free in order to appreciate another side of life.

The poet faces a number of challenges: he is reading an unpublished work that he has written out in a notebook. He is also unknown and unestablished, as is shown by his lack of a name in the story. While Pavlova was not in exactly the same situation, she understood the difficulties of being taken seriously as an artist and had to contend with the added obstacle of her gender. Both the poet in A Double Life and Pavlova experience a lack of appreciation for their creative translation work. In fact, Pavlova introduces the poem in such a way as to minimize the amount of credit given to her by the reader. She presents what is in fact her own adroit translation of Schiller as her fictional character's work and even interrupts his reading by shifting the narrative focus onto the audience and its response.

At this key moment in Cecily's life, Pavlova draws attention to what Lawrence Venuti has termed the "translator's invisibility."[13] The effect of a fluent translation is often to hide the work of the translator. Yet by examining the work of translation, we can recover a further creative layer to a work and shine a light on the different cultural contexts in which it is received.

NOTES

1. Karolina Pavlova, Polnoe sobranie stikhotvorenii (Moscow and Leningrad: Sovetskii pisatel', 1964), 231–307.
2. See, for example, Jehanne Gheith, "Women of the 1830s and 1850s: Alternative Periodizations," in A History of Women's Writing in Russia, ed. Adele Marie Barker and Jehanne M. Gheith (Cambridge: Cambridge University Press, 2002), 85–99.
3. "Dvoinaia zhizn'. Ocherk. K. Pavlovoi.," "Literaturnaia letopis'," Biblioteka dlia chteniia, no. 87 (1848): 2.

4. Baron Rozen, "Dvoinaia zhizn'. *Ocherk. Soch. K. Pavlovoi.*," "Kritika i bibliografiia," *Syn otechestva*, no. 5 (1848): 1.
5. Baron Rozen, "Dvoinaia zhizn'. *Ocherk. Soch. K. Pavlovoi.*," 3.
6. Catriona Kelly, *A History of Russian Women's Writing 1820–1992* (Oxford: Oxford University Press, 1998), 41.
7. "Dvoinaia zhizn'. Ocherk. K. Pavlovoi," *Sovremennik*, 47.
8. V. Belinskii, "Vstuplenie", *Fiziologiia Peterburga*, ed. Nikolai Nekrasov (St. Petersburg: Bookseller A. Ivanov's Publisher, 1845), 26.
9. Diana Greene discusses this in Diana Greene, "Gender and Genre in Karolina Pavlova's *A Double Life,*" *Slavic Review* 54, no. 3 (Autumn, 1995), 572.
10. Brian Baer, *Translation and the Making of Modern Russian Literature* (New York: Bloomsbury, 2016), 90.
11. Daria Khitrova, "Neizvestnyi stikh Baratynskogo," *Tynianovskii sbornik* (2006): 12:210.
12. Diana Greene, *Reinventing Romantic Poetry* (Madison: University of Wisconsin Press, 2004), 36.
13. Lawrence Venuti, *The Translator's Invisibility: A History of Translation* (New York: Routledge, 1995).

R THE RUSSIAN LIBRARY

Between Dog and Wolf by Sasha Sokolov, translated by Alexander Boguslawski

Strolls with Pushkin by Andrei Sinyavsky, translated by Catharine Theimer Nepomnyashchy and Slava I. Yastremski

Fourteen Little Red Huts and Other Plays by Andrei Platonov, translated by Robert Chandler, Jesse Irwin, and Susan Larsen

Rapture: A Novel by Iliazd, translated by Thomas J. Kitson

City Folk and Country Folk by Sofia Khvoshchinskaya, translated by Nora Seligman Favorov

Writings from the Golden Age of Russian Poetry by Konstantin Batyushkov, presented and translated by Peter France

Found Life: Poems, Stories, Comics, a Play, and an Interview by Linor Goralik, edited by Ainsley Morse, Maria Vassileva, and Maya Vinokur

Sisters of the Cross by Alexei Remizov, translated by Roger John Keys and Brian Murphy

Sentimental Tales by Mikhail Zoshchenko, translated by Boris Dralyuk

Redemption by Friedrich Gorenstein, translated by Andrew Bromfield

The Man Who Couldn't Die: The Tale of an Authentic Human Being by Olga Slavnikova, translated by Marian Schwartz

Necropolis by Vladislav Khodasevich, translated by Sarah Vitali

Nikolai Nikolaevich and Camouflage: Two Novels, by Yuz Aleshkovsky, translated by Duffield White, edited by Susanne Fusso

New Russian Drama: An Anthology, edited by Maksim Hanukai and Susanna Weygandt